WHITE LIGHTNING

HOPE SZE MEDICAL CRIME 9

MELISSA YI

*For Dr. Foley,
Happy holidays
and best wishes for
2022!
cheers,
M*

Windtree
Press

Dedicated to N

Join Melissa's mailing list at www.melissayuaninnes.com

Copyright © 2021 by Melissa Yuan-Innes

Published by Olo Books in association with Windtree Press

Yi, Melissa, author   White Lightning / Melissa Yi.
(Hope Sze crime novel; 9)
Issued in print and electronic formats.
ISBN 978-1-927341-98-8 (softcover).--ISBN 978-1-927341-97-1 (eBook)
    I. Title.   C813'.6

All rights reserved.

No part of this book may be reproduced in any form or by any electronic or mechanical means, including information storage and retrieval systems, without written permission from the author, except for the use of brief quotations in a book review.

This is a work of fiction. Names, characters, institutions, organizations, corporations, locales or events in this novel are either the result of the author's imagination or, if real, used fictitiously. Any resemblance to actual persons, living or dead, is coincidental. This novel portrays medical crises and death and includes sexual situations and frank language.

To advise of typographical errors, please contact olobooks@gmail.com

I like to have a martini,
    Two at the very most.
    After three I'm under the table,
    After four I'm under my host.

— DOROTHY PARKER

You can get much farther with a kind word and a gun than you can with a kind word alone.

— AL CAPONE

Everything in life is about sex, except sex, which is about power.

— OSCAR WILDE

PROLOGUE
EDWIN

St Elizabeth's Orphanage of Mercy

~

Death stalked Edwin Jenkins.
    Edwin wasn't aware of that yet. For the moment, he knew only that the orphanage cook had burned their soup dry again tonight.

Edwin stepped on the crate that made him tall enough to crouch over the cast iron cooking pot on the kitchen counter. He picked out the burnt bits of potato and carrot crusted on the pot bottom, trying not to inhale.

"Hurry up!" called John, who had claimed the forks and spoons, the easiest washing-up.

Edwin started, wobbling on his crate. He grabbed the wood block counter. He kept his balance, but pain streaked through his right hand, which had cramped with cold.

They were both six years old, or so Mrs. Albury told them. Mrs. Albury ran the orphanage. She was old but quick with a switch, so Edwin tried to stay out of her way as much as he could.

Through the thin shared plaster wall, Edwin could hear Mrs. Albury raise her voice in the neighboring parlour. He couldn't make out her words, but as long as she didn't rush in scolding them, they were probably all right.

Edwin flinched as he rubbed the pot bottom with a rag dipped in ashes and vinegar. The vinegar stung the cracks in his hands.

Meanwhile, John pressed his ear against the wall so he could hear Mrs. Albury better. John escaped from punishment for things like that in a way that Edwin never would.

Edwin scoured the pot using white brick dust. Red brick dust sometimes left a stain, as he'd learned before another beating.

When John made a strange noise, Edwin glanced up from his pot.

John had always been the brave one, the loudest six-year-old at the orphanage. Edwin had never before seen John's lips tremble with fear.

"We're dead," John whispered.

1

WINDSOR, ONTARIO, CANADA

HOPE

"Hope, I've seen a ghost," said Tori Yamamoto.

"What? Are you serious?" I stepped back instead of kissing her on each cheek the way French Canadians do. Then I cautiously surveyed our surroundings, the attic bar of the Rumrunner's Rest, in Windsor, Ontario.

From the outside, the inn looked like an ordinary, two-story wood building—almost like two big houses constructed back to back—with a river view from the front. Well-maintained and stately, not spectral.

Inside the attic bar, between the wooden walls, the exposed rafter beams, the long slab wood tables, and each chair back made from a longitudinal slice of log, I couldn't help wondering how many trees had been killed for this place. We'd also had to creep down and then up a set of narrow spiral wooden staircases, and now the attic walls sloped inward at the edges, making me feel like I should crouch even though I'm a short woman, thanks to my Asian genes (five foot two and a quarter, thank you very much).

The Rumrunner's Rest was apparently quite the party house back in the Prohibition days. I wouldn't have picked it for our one weekend off, but my quirky fiancé, John Tucker, insisted we head here.

Tucker, Tori, and I are all resident physicians, or what used to be called interns, in Montreal, Canada. Tucker had persuaded us to come here on a rare weekend off for the three of us, and Tori had invited her mysterious new boyfriend, Griffin.

"Where did you see a ghost?" I asked Tori, smiling in case it was a joke. I'd never spotted any spirits in my life before and didn't want to start now.

She gestured for me to keep my voice down, even though the brunette bartender and her few customers hardly cared. A 60-ish guy with an unfortunate combover studied his empty glass while two older women in yellow shirts toasted each other.

"Yeah, I'm curious too. Let me grab us a drink first," said Tucker, swiping his fingers through his platinum blond hair before heading for the bar. He'd cut back on his gel and felt self-conscious about his floppier bangs, especially after we'd gotten caught in the rain en route.

"Isn't it weird that their bar is upstairs? I figured they'd hide it in a basement during Prohibition," I told Tucker.

"They needed maximum warning about police raids to give them time to cover up." Tucker winked at me, and I marvelled at the long, pale eyelashes framing his brown eyes. "So all the bars were upstairs. This one had the added security of the up and down staircases on the way in. They also had lookouts posted in their upstairs windows."

Tucker hurried toward the wood bar located directly across from the entrance. I smiled at the thigh high boot mounted above the bar, but raised my eyebrows at the single naked breast made of ceramic mounted to the right of the bottles of alcohol.

A century later, bootlegging seemed dashing, but this was the site of past crimes. Maybe even murders. Hence Tori's ghost, which she still hadn't explained.

Ugh. Ghosts schmosts. I shook off my superstition, or tried to. It's an Asian thing. Although evidence-based medicine rules my world, I still don't seek out the number four, after I heard that it sounds like the word death in Chinese.

Chapter 1

The address for the Rumrunner's Rest is #4 Riverside Drive. Just sayin'.

"Hi, are you here for Rogue Con?" asked the smiley brunette bartender whose name tag said Jennifer. I liked her freckles, prominent nose, and slightly uneven teeth.

Tucker snapped his fingers. "I heard about that! It's at the Four Candles downtown, isn't it?"

"Rogue Con?" Tori raised her eyebrows.

I screwed up my face. "I've heard of cons. Like a convention?" Medical conventions, which we call conferences, keep us on the cutting edge of medical research and treatment. They're also an excuse to drink and travel.

"Exactly," said Tucker, "only small and Canadian and random."

"And all about rogues?" I asked.

"Yeah. Bad guys. And girls. Villains."

"Why would I purposely spend my vacation with a bunch of bad guys?" I asked. Tucker had sold me Windsor with a combination of Lake Erie Beach and the world's best pizza. No villains required.

"They're all fictional villains. Strictly for fun. And they're staying at the Four Candles," Tucker said.

"A few con guests have relocated here," Jennifer informed us, with a smile. "We have a treat for all of you downstairs, if you care to follow me."

"What kind of treat?" I asked, but Tori had already fallen into step behind Jennifer while a bearded man took over the bar.

"Where's Griffin? I want to meet him," I told Tori.

She shook her head, her shiny black bob undulating in a way that mine never would. "He texted me. He told me to come see Javier, who's already filming in the basement."

"Who's that?"

"A TV host. They call him 'Windsor's Witness' because he covers the best local news stories."

A witness to what? Tucker literally rubbed his hands with glee, undeterred. "I love old places."

I laughed and patted his back. "You think this is part of the tour?" I whispered as we followed Tori.

"No, Griffin and I already did the tour earlier," Tori said.

"Shouldn't they let us buy drinks first?"

Jen grinned at me over her shoulder. "You can still order drinks. I'll call them up and a server will bring them down for you as 'one of the most beautiful, natural, wholesome things that money can buy.'"

"Hey, I know that quote. Can I have a gin and tonic?" A grey-haired woman giggled behind me.

"Great idea, Joan. Make it two! And throw in some tiger tail ice cream if you've got it!" cheered her friend in a gravelly smoker's voice. They both wore matching mustard-coloured Camp Crystal Lake T-shirts that outlined their love handles, not in a bad way.

I smiled at them, even though money-wise, Jennifer should've taken our drink orders first, then brought us downstairs while we were half tiddly.

"Two G&T's for Joan and Kathy," Jennifer said. "The ice cream's in our dining room. But I've got some fantastic mixed drinks, including the Bee's Knees. And have you ever tried Hope Diamond gin?"

I raised my eyebrows.

Tucker touched my shoulder. "Coincidence," he murmured. "I bet there aren't any diamonds in it, either."

"Probably a safe bet." I wrinkled my nose as we descended a second darkened set of wooden stairs behind the bar that creaked under our weight.

Jennifer grinned at us, undeterred. "Want more options? My personal favourite is White Lightning, our special brand of white whisky made famous in South Carolina."

Tucker grinned back. "You mean moonshine?"

"Yes, that's its other nickname, because it was produced at night. But as you can imagine, lots of different liquor was called moonshine. This one is special." Jennifer smiled at me. "If I may suggest, you'd like a Bearcat. It's fierce but delicious."

Tucker immediately agreed to both. Tori demurred, even though

Chapter 1

Kathy egged her on. "You've got to live a little! Look at us! We know how to party."

"Absolutely," said Tori politely.

We made our way into the musty basement, down a thin, dark hall before lining up at the door into what I assumed was the original furnace room.

A male voice resonated behind us, making Kathy and Joan squeal, but it was a handsome server with a man bun and a goatee, holding a trayful of drinks. "I hear some refreshments are in order!"

Joan leered at the server as she accepted her gin and tonic. "You know what Jennifer said?"

Kathy bellowed with laughter. *"I* know. It's a Steve Martin quote. *'Sex* is one of the most beautiful, natural, wholesome things that money can buy.'"

Joan winked at the guy and downed her drink. "Funny guy, right, Kathy?"

Kathy laughed so hard that she snorted her drink. The server smiled and bowed at them, seemingly unruffled.

I apologized with my eyes as the man handed me my amber Bearcat. Sexual harassment, hardee ha ha. The server raised his eyebrow in acknowledgement before passing the next glass to Tucker.

Tucker and I shared a silent toast, then drank as we filed into a small, dark room already filled with over a dozen people.

Mistake. The alcohol in that Bearcat ripped at my throat and roared up my nose. I choked but managed to keep it down as several people, including some winner wearing a white face mask, glanced over their shoulders and distanced themselves from me.

"Wow," said Tori.

I coughed, eyes watering, while Tucker patted my back and said, "Appropriate for a Bearcat."

I nodded but tried for another sip, even though my throat kept spasming. The liquid threatened to slosh out of my glass.

Finally, I got it under control and managed another small sip. And a third.

"You tamed the Bearcat," said Tori, eyeing me.

I giggled, slightly lightheaded already. My ex-boyfriend, Ryan Wu, used to laugh at how fast I'd get buzzed. Was it hot in this little basement, or was it just me?

Tucker kissed my cheek. I could tell he wanted to pat me on the head. "You want some White Lightning, Hope?"

"Hell, no."

He took a sip of my Bearcat—"Not bad. She's fierce!"—while Tori pivoted slowly on her heel, her eyes moving up and down what looked like mold marking the concrete walls, highlighted when someone turned on a very bright light.

I tried not to breathe too deeply as they dangled a microphone over the man in the spotlight. I sidled next to Tori and offered her a sip of my reclaimed Bearcat. She shook her head.

"Will you tell me about the ghost?" I whispered.

Tori shook her head and pressed a finger to her lips while Jen told the camera, "A local college professor and amateur historian, Marina Ma, has arranged a special surprise for the guests of the Rumrunner's Rest. I'll let Javier explain the rest."

Javier was the spotlighted man, a thirtyish white male journalist with black-framed glasses and a shaved head in a burgundy suit and a bow tie. Somehow he managed not to look ridiculous as he faced the cameraman and said, "Thank you, Jennifer. Marina and her partner, Ryan, noticed something strange when they investigated the blueprints for this very building, the Rumrunner's Rest."

Wait a minute. Did he say *Ryan?*

I clocked Tucker's rigid shoulders and Tori's compressed lips. Yes, he did say Ryan. I wasn't drunkenly hallucinating.

Oh, well. Of the millions of Ryans in the world, only one was my first and most pure love. I'm not supposed to love two people at once, so I let him go. He blocked me. Now I'm engaged to Tucker and conforming to monogamy like a good girl.

I tried to check out the room, unobtrusively, for Ryan Wu. I felt both relieved and agonized not to find him.

Then I noticed Tucker scowling as he scoped the 20-odd faces surrounding us. Which made me drink in earnest as Javier's voice filled the room.

"They believe that this bricked-off chimney, the one in front of your very eyes, contains something of interest to Prohibition historians around the world."

Tori froze in place.

2

I squinted at the brick chimney now spotlighted behind Javier. Yep, I could make out the brick surround built into the wall. Someone had used darker red brick to fill in what I think is called the hearth, the mouth of the fireplace where you'd normally lay the firewood.

Jennifer had brought us down so they could dismantle this chimney in front of a boozed-up live audience. Why? What did they think they might find?

Tori swung around to face the wall to our left. I tried to distract her by whispering, "Tell me about the ghost instead."

She shook her head and pulled out her phone, probably to text Griffin, the mystery boyfriend.

Now that I thought about it, no Griffin had come to greet us. Who was he, and how did he end up in the basement ahead of us?

I shouldn't have to worry about Tori. She soldiered on when everyone else complained about working 24/7 while our hospital literally fell to pieces around us (seriously, the plaster crumbled off the stairwell walls).

She was a calm, highly intelligent physician who neatly turned attention away from herself, except for her eye-catching ink sketches.

She wouldn't mention ghosts lightly, and she shouldn't give her heart away to someone who didn't deserve it. She was an island unto herself. Hell, I had no clue about her boyfriend's existence until she said that Griffin should come this weekend.

Tucker took my hand with a tiny head shake. He wanted me to leave Tori alone.

I awarded him a perfunctory smile, squeezed his hand back, and used my free hand to text Tori. *What's wrong?*

She read the text, but stuck her phone back in her pocket instead of answering me.

Javier raised his voice. "Please welcome Ms. Marina Ma, a business professor at Chester College, and our guide to bootlegger history tonight!"

I raised my eyebrows at Tori, but she cooly ignored me, joining in the applause.

I clapped too as the small crowd parted to allow a pretty blonde to trot down the stairs in stilettos. As she passed me, I noted her Asian eyes, but she was otherwise everything I wasn't: tall, voluntarily wearing a black pantsuit and heels, effortlessly thin, with big tits—how was that fair?

Javier waved away Kathy and Joan to make room for Marina at his side. "Hello, Marina. You and Ryan aren't architects or historians. What made you study bootlegging at the Rumrunner's Rest?"

Tori finally texted me back. *I can't tell you.*

I shook my head, letting go of Tucker so I could text with both hands. *You can tell me anything.*

Meanwhile, professor Marina's high voice filled the small room: "Rumrunning, Javier. The illegal transport of alcohol is called bootlegging when it's done over land, because people would hide flasks in their boots. But when you transport that alcohol over water, as was done from Windsor to Detroit, that's called rumrunning."

"Touché! I stand corrected, professor!" Javier mugged for the camera. "I do know that most illegal booze heading from Canada to the US made its way over the Detroit River."

"Yes, 75 percent of all illegal alcohol that made its way into the States came right through here. It was called Hooch Highway."

Joan and Kathy cackled and applauded.

"That's also why Detroit was ground zero for Prohibition officers. Even to this day, on this side of the border, the RCMP is stationed on the river."

"How do you know all that? Was that part of your MBA?" asked Javier.

"I teach business at Chester College, but history is one of my passions, especially the Rumrunner's Rest."

Javier held his hand up. "Amen! The Bearcat could knock your socks off. Am I right?"

She high-fived him and grinned. "Yes. And one of my students, Wy Leighton, found the Rumrunner's Rest's blueprints. My partner Ryan and I noticed the non-functional chimney, and he bought a phone app that scans behind walls."

An app that can see behind walls? Weird. But no weirder than an app that can create an EKG, I guess.

My phone buzzed with a text from Tori. *No. You'd think I'm crazy.*

I texted my answer and mouthed it at her to boot. *Never.*

She closed her eyes.

"An app that scans behind walls," said Javier. "That's a new one on me. Ryan—oh, there you are. Come on in. You're an engineer, aren't you? Could you explain that app?"

Dafuq.

Ryan. The engineer.

I rotated to stare at the bottom of the stairs, and sure enough, Ryan Wu, my Ryan Wu, the former light of my life, began walking toward me.

I have never fainted before. The closest I came was when I joined an evening ballet barre class on an empty stomach and my vision started to go black at the edges.

I fought against the same blackness now while my skin prickled and a scream built in my chest.

Tori's eyes widened, and Tucker wrapped his arms around me

from behind. I squeezed my eyelids shut and leaned against Tucker, but my mind's eye replayed Ryan's black hair, a little longer in the front and short on the sides. Brown eyes that stared straight into your soul. That long, lean runner's build.

Breaking up with me hadn't made him fat. It had netted him an Asian blonde business professor/amateur historian with D cups. What the what.

To make it more unfair, Ryan was wearing some sort of pin-striped suit, a hat, and two-toned shoes. I'd never seen him in retro gear before. He should've looked like a buffoon, but instead he looked hotter than the California Reaper hot pepper we'd once tried on a dare.

Joan and Kathy stepped directly in front of me, blocking my vision, and my first reaction was to behead them.

"Jesus!" I said out loud.

The women glanced at me, but I popped up on my toes to gaze in the resulting gap between their heads.

Ryan's head swivelled toward me. He never did appreciate me taking the Lord's name in vain.

Ten feet away from each other, our gazes locked and loaded. I couldn't make out his expression under that hat.

Tucker squeezed my ribs so hard that it hurt, and I wanted it to. I let the air out of my lungs as the interviewer blathered away and Marina tugged on Ryan's arm.

Don't touch my man.

Tori glanced at me as if I'd spoken aloud.

Tucker pressed his cheek against mine. I inhaled his soapy smell. *I'm here. With Tucker. And Tori. Now.*

Ryan turned to Javier, his voice even. "Have you ever used stud finders? This app combines scanning with a thermal camera. It shows the different densities of different construction materials."

"What does that mean, in English?" Javier winked at the camera.

"I can see different materials and different temperatures." Ryan paused. "I even saw movement behind the bricks."

"*Movement* behind the wall!" Javier pretended to shudder. "You don't think something or some*one* is trapped behind there, do you?"

"It was probably mice," said Ryan.

Most of us relaxed—hey, better than Tori's ghost—but one of the middle-aged women, Kathy, broke the silence with her raspy voice. "Oh, my goodness. Mice! I cannot abide vermin!"

That broke me out of my spell. I stuffed back a laugh. Who talks like that?

But also, who wants to corral a bunch of people into a room and rip open that chimney to release a bunch of mice at our feet? They must think there was something pretty spectacular behind that brick.

Joan towed Kathy toward the stairs, their yellow shirts obvious even in the dim light away from Javier.

"You okay?" Tucker loosened his grip on me to offer them a hand, but they trundled right by him, clinging to their drinks. A handsome, dark-skinned man descending the stairs drew back to give them room.

More people spilled down the stairway, some of them in costume. Well, the combover dude wore a faded brown suit that might or might not be a costume, but I was pretty sure that the fortyish woman wouldn't normally strut around in a G string and pasties.

Although she seemed less alarming than the teenager who wore only a bra and underwear covered in cotton balls. And what about the ripped guy with all visible skin dyed blue? That was a lot of skin, because he only seemed to be wearing a pretend diaper.

As the cameraman panned over these Rogue Con refugees, G String Lady posed with her hands on her hips. Then she winked and pretended to spank the blue guy, who stepped away and frowned at her—consent, ma'am!—while the white face mask man hovered behind them.

I exhaled and muttered, "Is Hitler coming too? Bad idea."

"No, Hitler and Nazis are against the rules," Tucker said seriously. "Everyone's a fake bad guy who's never massacred anyone. They banned Stalin, Mao, and Pol Pot too."

"Little pig, little pig, let me in!" a guy bellowed from the top of the stairs, and more Rogues laughed as they continued to snake into the basement, one of them pulling the fries out of his poutine while his buddy scarfed a cinnamon donut and said, "This is better than a Spitfires game!"

"Now don't be talking sacrilege," said a third guy in a hockey shirt, so I guessed that was a hockey team.

"Welcome, visitors!" Javier waved at the Rogues and turned back to Ryan. "Meanwhile, you've been checking out the chimney. What did you see?"

Ryan grimaced. "The app isn't great. It can't penetrate too deeply."

Stud finder. Penetrate.

I shook myself. *Get a hold of yourself, Hope Sze.*

Ryan and Tucker both half-turned toward me as if they could hear my lascivious thoughts. I sipped my drink to cover up my burning cheeks.

Marina's teensy voice took over. "From what we saw, we believe that something is bricked in behind the chimney."

Blue Guy yelled, "But what is it?"

3

"That's exactly what you'll find out tonight!" Javier spread his arms. "Every one of you will bear witness. Is it a relic from Prohibition? Some ancient bottles? Or is it something even more obscure? What do you think, professor?"

"I have my suspicions." Marina dimpled at him. I decided her bilateral dimples should be illegal. Just looking out for her. I mean, her students might not take her seriously.

"Originally, the Rumrunner's Rest was called the Dreamland Inn, first built in 1920 to take advantage of Prohibition," said Javier.

"You do know your history," Marina said, Javier beamed, and I rolled my eyes.

"I obtained permission from the current owners to open the chimney tonight," said Marina. "It's a big decision, but they're historians too. They want to know what might be behind that chimney."

"So do we," said Javier.

The blue guy pumped his fist in the air in agreement, and when the cameraman panned over them, G String shook her breasts at him.

"Well, you certainly have the audience for it! We have a few guests from Rogue Con and from the Rumrunner's Rest tonight." Javier gestured, and the cameraman now focused on our tiny crew.

I casually lifted my hand to block my face and left it there until Tucker nudged me to let me know I was safe. I wished I'd brought a hat like Ryan, or a wig like Sia, so I could go out incognito.

The tall, dark, and handsome man, whom I'd noticed earlier avoiding Joan and Kathy, also tilted his head away from the camera as he wove through the crowd toward us.

To my surprise, Tori took the man's hand, and he bent over to whisper something in her ear. She nodded seriously.

So this was Griffin. Tori hadn't mentioned that her guy was—Black? Yes, I thought so, with his melanin and a strong nose, but his eyes looked Asian. Normally I don't ask people's ethnicities because I'm sick of strangers yelling "Ni hao!" at me, but this guy's features fascinated me, even without blue makeup.

No, no, no. Bad Hope. I swung my gaze back to Tucker. My funny, wild fiancé. The guy I promised to love and cherish whenever we had time to plan a wedding.

Tucker thunked his empty glass down on a side table I hadn't noticed next to the concrete wall on our left. That sound echoed throughout the room, and he left a gap between him and me when he rejoined us.

I wanted to explain that I hadn't seen or spoken to Ryan since December. Almost four whole months. Because Ryan had blocked me, but no one should dwell on that.

"We can leave," I murmured to Tucker, ignoring a new guy in a hard hat who had started explaining to Javier what a lintel was and how he'd started dismantling the fireplace earlier this week, but had left the last pieces in place until now.

Tucker shook his head, pushing his way to the front of the crowd for a better view.

I hung back, even though a dozen inconvenient heads filled my view. My head swirled, and I carefully placed my own half-filled glass on the side table.

My ex-boyfriend held center stage, my fiancé was jealous, and they were opening up a mouse-laden chimney in front of my drunken face. I needed all my neurons intact.

I wasn't too tipsy to notice that the construction guy had already loosened the bricks before, so now all he had to do was wiggle them out, one at a time. This was a show.

Jennifer joined Javier's side. "On behalf of the Rumrunner's Rest, I'd like to thank our sponsors, especially the Mackenzie Corporation and the Grant Foundation. They both made a generous donation to STIP, Stop Trafficking in People, an organization close to my heart. My goal is to stop human trafficking in and around Windsor, especially in hotels."

Oh. At least this was for a good cause. One of my police officer friends, Arabella Visser, had explained that human trafficking includes any forced exploitation of people. Everyone thinks of white sex slaves, but the most common method is actually forced farm labour. Horrible any way you slice it.

I applauded along with everyone else. Tucker whistled.

Weird that the Mackenzie Corporation had sponsored it, though. They're North America's largest online retailer, notorious for forcing local Mom and Pop shops to close because everyone clicks for direct shipping instead of walking down the street.

Believe me, I have never seen the Mackenzie Corp give anything to charity, let alone something like STIP. Their warehouse workers end up peeing in bottles because they don't have time for a proper bathroom break.

"Mackenzie, the Grant Foundation, and an anonymous donor made this event possible today." Jennifer held up a placard with Mackenzie logo, with a fire burning over the I, and an X under the company name. I remembered hearing that Mackenzie means "born of fire" in Gaelic.

Well, maybe Mackenzie was trying to kickstart their image after the bad publicity of them union busting and dodging taxes. Entirely possible.

Javier kept up a steady patter. "Thank you, Mackenzie, for sponsoring this fascinating night! What's behind this brick wall? Nobody knows! This wall has been sealed for decades. We could be breathing the same air as the Prohibition agents and the bootleggers! I mean rumrunners!"

I stifled a laugh. The air part could have been true. After we came back from Egypt, I'd heard a podcast about the secret chamber in King Tutankhamun's tomb. It was so well-sealed that they hadn't discovered it until recently, and they debated about how best to open it. They wanted to study the air that had been sealed for thousands of years. It might be our last chance to analyze ancient air.

Still, Prohibition ended in what, 1933? Less than a century ago. The air shouldn't have been so different then. Any pre-loosened bricks would allow air to escape. Plus what if the chimney was still open on top?

Even so, we all leaned forward.

Ryan held his phone up, thermal camera attached, app engaged. "There's no movement now. Any mice must have been scared away. Still, if you can see what I'm looking at, there's a shape, here ... "

He held up his phone to Javier and the cameraman. There was no way I could see it, but the crowd murmured.

"Look at that!"

"Hello!"

"I wonder what it is?"

I rolled my eyes. Most likely, they *wanted* to see something. The power of suggestion. Like when Tucker showed me YouTube videos of records played backwards. Sheer gobblygook until the narrator tells you what they're saying, and then I clearly heard "Satan is good."

The chimney was probably full of nothing but an old bird's nest.

Except that Marina and Ryan had convinced the owners to pay a guy to open up the chimney, with a local TV celebrity playing host and a crowd of rogues cheering them on.

It meant that Ryan believed. And he doesn't lie. Partly it's his religion, partly it's his nature. He doesn't like publicity, and he's careful, not flashy. If he thought there was something in there, I'd bet my money the same way.

I took Tucker's hand again. After a minute, he squeezed my

fingers. I squeezed back, knowing his inner war: he'd love to discover a historical artifact, but he'd revel in Ryan's humiliation if they came up empty.

A low sound thrummed through the room, which made the cotton ball girl jump. And me too, to be honest.

Then I recognized the sound, a drum beating out a smooth rhythm that accelerated our heart rates.

A slim Black man, maybe 20 years old, emerged from the shadows at the front of the room, to the right of the fireplace. The cameraman focused in on him and his drum, and the blue guy moved closer to see him.

The drum itself didn't look like much, a circular piece of skin on a pedestal-like base, held between his legs, but the sounds he got out of it!

The bass beats echoed through the room and seemed to thunder in my heart. The higher slaps raised the hair on my arms.

Some women started dancing, but I could hardly breathe as the construction guy removed the bricks more and more quickly, leaving the last one for Marina to ceremoniously remove.

Tori brushed her hand in front of her nose, and I realized there was an odd smell. Something fetid and damp, with a definite eau de olden days.

Marina carried the last red brick in both hands, almost like it was a treasure. She set it on a pile on top of the others.

Like a pyramid, I thought, and my mind flipped to Egypt again. We'd mostly had a good time except that an unknown stalker had come after me. He shouldn't bother following me to Canada. Still, I took the precaution of avoiding cameras, and I'd disabled the social media presence my little brother had created for me.

"And now! The moment you've all been waiting for. What has been hidden here for almost a century?" The drum beats reverberated off the walls. Javier shouted to be heard above their commanding beat. "What was hidden so cleverly for decades in this chimney? Is it money? Is it moonshine? Or is it nothing at all?"

Brick dust and bad air, I thought wildly. That Bearcat drink had gotten the best of me, and I wanted to lie down, but the drumbeat thundered as Ryan shone a safety light into the fireplace opening.

That smell again. I almost choked.

I couldn't see. I surged forward, but so did everyone else, people knotted together, their heads bent, their arms pinned to their sides.

"What's happening?" I yelled, and then someone screamed.

"What is it? I'm a doctor," I called.

Strangely, Tori's new boyfriend answered. His height allowed him to peer over the crowd's heads and say, "It's too late for a doctor. Those are bones."

4

EDWIN

Dead? What did John mean, dead?
Edwin opened his mouth to ask, but John darted out of the kitchen, toward the dormitories.

Edwin stared after him, still clutching the pot in his hand, when Mrs. Albury hurried into the kitchen through the opposite door, her lips turned upward in a smile that vanished as soon as she set eyes on him. "Edwin. Where did John go?"

"I don't know."

She sighed in exasperation. "Anyway, you'll do. You're the same size. Come on, then."

Edwin shook his head. He hadn't finished the washing-up.

Mrs. Albury yanked the pot out of Edwin's hand, tossed his cleaning rag on the table, and smoothed his hair before she jerked him behind her, bringing him into the parlour.

A thin man stood in front of the fire. The most startling thing about him was that most of his face and hands were as black as the pot bottom Edwin had been scouring, although his eyes were light blue like Edwin's.

Those chilly eyes set themselves on Edwin, surveying him up and down.

Chapter 4

Mrs. Albury spoke in a soft voice Edwin had never heard before. "Mr. Bagnell, this is Edwin Jenkins. Hard-working lad. No trouble at all."

Mrs. Albury's voice, as well as her sweet smile fixed on Mr. Bagnell, made Edwin shudder even before the man growled, "You said his name was John."

Edwin didn't understand. His name had always been Edwin. His nan said it was a good name, a strong name that would bring him luck.

Every day, he prayed that his nan would come to the orphanage and take him home. That was all the luck he needed.

Mrs. Albury tittered, a high, startling sound. "Edwin's better than John, Mr. Bagnell. One of the best boys at the orphanage. I'm sure you can call him John if you like, Mr. Bagnell."

Edwin studied his shoes, trying not to breathe or move too deeply. He understood now. This man, this dirty man, might take him away. He couldn't let that happen. Please, no.

Mr. Bagnell screwed up his face like he'd bitten his tongue.

Edwin wiggled his toes and prayed that the man would keep asking for John.

Mr. Bagnell began circling Edwin in a way that a lion might stalk its prey. Edwin had never seen a lion, but John had told stories about them, and Edwin could imagine a big cat padding around him with his enormous paws. Its presence and its power alone froze him in place. He could smell the beer and feel the heat of Mr. Bagnell's breath.

Then Mr. Bagnell grabbed Edwin's arms, squeezing them like he was checking the freshness of a loaf of bread.

Edwin gasped before Mrs. Albury's eye fell on him, and Edwin quickly snapped his mouth shut.

Come back, John.

5

HOPE

The drummer stopped, leaving an odd silence.

Ignoring the uneasy atmosphere, I craned my neck, but I couldn't make anything out except the audience's heads and backs and elbows.

The white mask man slowly began to clap.

"All right!" The pizza guy joined him before more murmurs took over.

"What the hell?"

"This is trippy."

"Is this part of Rogue Con?"

"Let me see!" piped a small voice.

My heart banged in my chest. Last month, we unsuccessfully ran a code on a toddler. I have to practice acting normal around kids again.

Luckily, instead of a child, I saw a babyish woman with red cheeks and black hair dressed like a manga character.

The others at the back muttered their agreement, but at least six people filming mutely in the front row refused to stir.

Since Griffin had a clear view of the bones, I asked him, "Are they real?"

Chapter 5

Tucker twisted around to stare at me. "I don't know if we should examine them."

"Right. We probably shouldn't touch them," I said. We're doctors. So far, my only patients had been alive.

"We should call the police," said Tori.

I nodded. The police. That made sense. They took care of dead bodies. They must take care of bones too.

"Shouldn't we make sure they're real first?" Tucker asked.

"And that they're human bones," said Griffin. It was only the second time I'd heard him speak, but both times, he'd made very good points.

"Sure. We don't want to call the police for nothing," I said, and then I noticed the cameraman filming us. I turned away with my hand over my face.

"So you're voting to touch the bones," said Tucker.

"No, I'm voting against. Don't contaminate them."

"Locard's Principle," said Griffin.

"Yes, exactly." I raised my eyebrows and smiled at him. Tori had definitely picked an unusual guy. After the chaos, I looked forward to getting to know him.

Tori explained to the crowd around us, and therefore to the camera, "Dr. Edmond Locard's Exchange Principle points out that two objects coming into contact necessitates a transfer of material."

"That's so interesting," said Javier. "Can you translate that for regular folk?"

Tucker nodded. "It's impossible for a killer to come into a room without leaving a trace behind. Maybe it's as obvious as blood or a footprint or a hair. Maybe it's a microscopic piece of DNA. But no one comes in contact without leaving something behind."

"Even after a century?" Javier asked me. "What do you think?"

I pretended not to hear him. Tucker kept going. He and I had taken the same online forensic science course. "That's a good point. Old evidence may get lost over time, like shoe prints wiped away or clothes fibres blown into the hallway. But we'd certainly leave our own imprints behind if we approached the bones."

"I get it," said Javier. "If they find traces of micro fleece and Jägerbomb, they'll know it's not from Prohibition."

"And the evidence will be contaminated," said Tori. She'd taken the course after us. Maybe she'd passed some gems on to Griffin, although he still seemed surprisingly knowledgeable for a civilian.

"We should check if these are genuine human bones," Javier told us. "You said yourselves, we don't want to waste the police officers' time. And you're a doctor, you said. A medical doctor."

The four of us exchanged glances. Pushing us to examine the bones made for good TV but poor forensics.

"Well. The room around the fireplace has been open this entire time," Tucker said, loud enough for the camera to pick up. "And we're probably the only doctors here."

Ryan watched me. He and Marina had backed away from the fireplace, and now he was about nine feet away from me. It was still the closest we'd been since we broke up. My face burned, although I avoided looking at him.

"Did you say we? How many of you are doctors?" Javier's face lit up.

"I'm a family medicine resident. You can call me Tucker."

I bit my lip. Tucker had given his name on local TV. We'd popped up on the notoriety radar. Again.

"My colleagues prefer to remain anonymous," said Tucker as he made his way to the fireplace.

Javier followed him, talking the entire time. "Where do you practice?"

"We're studying in Montreal, Quebec."

"We're short of family doctors. I hope you'll consider practicing here when you're finished training."

"Absolutely. I've heard such good things about your cinnamon donuts and peach juice, you never know."

Griffin pulled out his phone so he could watch the footage in real time. Tori and I peered over his shoulder.

The cloth around the bones looked like it might be clothing, maybe made of grey wool. That alone made me think it was from a

Chapter 5

different era. We still wear wool, but not as often, and most people would avoid this kind of coarse weave nowadays.

Tucker stood a good two feet back. He didn't have to say anything.

A single long bone poked out of the wool. It looked like the end of a humerus.

6

"It looks human," said Tucker. "I won't come any closer. Please call the police."

"I will!" Javier took great delight in calling the police himself, live and on-camera.

"You okay, Hope?" asked Tucker, as he made our trio back into a quartet.

I nodded, but my mind locked on those bones.

If you asked me the worst way to die, I'd say it's a toss up between torture and fire.

Did someone die in this chimney?

I'd bet death by a thousand cuts was worse, because that can last three days. Seventy-two hours of agony, knowing the entire time that they might cart away your relatives next and torture them and their children the same way.

Burning to death should be faster. Maybe you'd die from suffocation first, but you can't count on that.

Dying in a chimney, plus or minus burning and suffocation would be pretty terrible.

"Don't think about it. Drink," said Tucker.

I grimaced, but that's one coping strategy, for sure. "I already got rid of it." I pointed out my glass on the table and turned to sober Tori, who still hadn't answered the ghost question. Unless these bones were the answer?

I don't believe in ghosts, but I don't disbelieve in them either. I keep an open mind. Ghosts are supposed to be restless spirits. This poor soul would've tried to send out a distress signal, kind of an all-points bulletin for sensitive live people to pick up.

Since I couldn't catch Tori's eye, I reached out to tap her shoulder.

Before I made contact, Tucker held up a familiar glass. "Do you want your drink? We can get more, but it'll take a while."

"No, thanks." My mild buzz had evaporated the second we found the bones.

I guess Tucker's had, too, because he gulped down the last of my Bearcat. He didn't cough, he didn't choke. He kept swallowing like he couldn't get enough.

I couldn't rip my eyes away. I'd never seen him funnel liquor like that before. I found myself worrying about him. Wondering what was going on under that bleached mop of his.

Tucker licked his lips and grinned at me, but I could tell he didn't mean it. Something was bothering him. Whether it was Ryan, the skeleton, or the Rogues, I couldn't blame him.

Griffin drew Tori into his chest as he watched the river of people pushing their way into the room. Our eyes met, and Griffin and I nodded at each other, recognizing a mutual sense of caution.

The blue guy tossed his arm around G String. She leaned toward him despite the smears of blue makeup on her bare shoulders. Maybe everyone needed comfort right now.

I kissed Tucker's ear. "I love you," I whispered, which he probably couldn't hear as a few people, then more and more of the audience, started to chant, "Show-the-*bones*. Show-the-*bones*."

Tucker whispered, "Me too" as my phone buzzed with a text from an unknown number, but it sounded like my brother Kevin. He's only nine years old and is the main person in my life addicted to emojis.

Hope! I got a phone! Did you see the 💀💀💀 bones? 👻💀

Me: *Kevin? Did Mom and Dad give you a new phone? How did you know about the bones?*

Kevin: 😎 💧 🫵 📿 🔥🔥🔥🔥🔥 🤩

Me: *Seriously, who told you?*

Kevin: *Mr. Ng. He's taking all of us out in his Zénobe for an epic steak dinner!*

I didn't care about electric cars, even the famous luxury brands like the Zénobe. I hadn't seen my brother in months and could use a free dinner, but I had a more important question.

Me: *Who's Mr. Ng?*

Kevin: *He's* 🔥*!*

I frowned at my phone.

Me: *Does he work with Dad or something?*

Kevin: 😜

Me: *What does that mean?*

Kevin didn't answer, but I had to pocket my phone when the police descended the stairs, parted the crowd, and got everyone to take five steps back, squishing us against other bodies. Some of us were pressed against the moldy walls. I got busy saying yes sir, no ma'am, and smiling assiduously at the police.

Luckily, the police didn't seem too upset about Tucker eyeing the bones in the chimney. The cameraman had taken extensive video of the potential humerus, but none of us had touched them or even come close.

"Thanks for staying back," said the female officer, whose badge said S. MAHONEY.

"No problem," I said, secretly wriggling in embarrassment because I'd only recently learned Locard's Principle.

The police didn't spend a lot of time interviewing us. It was pretty obvious that we had nothing to do with a bunch of bones that had probably been bricked up before our parents and even our great-grandparents were born.

The police talked to their radios and to each other. It sounded like they'd assigned a detective to the case, and she'd (yep, sounded like a woman) told them to call Coroner Dispatch.

"Patterson's on," a cop said, and I thought I saw another officer give an eye roll.

"Okay, I'm sure you kids want to get back to your party, right?" a cop said to Tucker.

My guy nodded, but his eyes were all over the chimney.

"If the bones are over 50 years old, it's not a police case," said S. Mahoney. "You kids go have fun. Enjoy yourselves while you can."

She meant it in a nice way, but Griffin twitched. I pressed my lips together in sympathy. Black Lives Matter has highlighted cases of the police killing unarmed Black men and children, and I knew why Griffin didn't find "while you can" so benign.

Tori placed her hand over Griffin's. "Maybe we'll go to the Rogue Con opening ball. I heard they're moving it here from their hotel because of a small fire at the Four Candles."

A fire? That was strange, but S. Mahoney nodded in agreement. "The fire has been contained."

Before I could ask about that, Tucker smiled at her. "Strong work. We shouldn't keep you. Can you keep in touch, though?" He took the officers' cards and thanked them, shaking their hands and telling them how much he admired the officers who helped us out in the emergency department.

Meanwhile, I waved goodbye and retreated, patting my jeans pocket to make sure I had our room key. *Skeleton key*, my mind whispered as I pulled out our car keys.

"What's that?" asked Griffin, pointing at the fluorescent pink doohickey on my keychain.

"It's a CarResCue. It cuts seatbelts and can break car windows in an emergency."

Griffin raised his eyebrows, but I didn't care. I'd bought one for each of us. Tori held her lime green one in the air as evidence.

"It only takes 22 pounds of force to asphyxiate a toddler, and a car's windows can exert anywhere from 30 to 80 pounds of force," I told him. "We're also all registered on Finding Friends, a tracking app."

"Why don't you use WhatsApp?" Griffin asked while some Rogue Conner dressed as an old lady nudged toward us and stopped dead.

7

"Since you're looking for old bones ... " she called in a creaky voice.

That made me take a closer look at Grandma Moses. She was no twenty-something trying out Instagram aging makeup and white-not-greige hair twisted in a bun.

There was something too genuine about the way her head thrust forward atop her curved spine, and she shuffled her feet on the ground with a right-sided limp that wasn't hidden by a floral blue and white nightgown.

This 75-year-old passed me by without so much as a sniff, so that she could crane her neck up at Tucker, who was finally waving farewell to the police.

"I thought so," said the old lady with satisfaction.

Tucker bowed at the waist. He's nice to old people. And almost all people, I guess, but something about seniors brings on his European gentleman mode.

The lady's eyes sparkled behind her glasses. "I found you, White Lightning."

Griffin and I exchanged glances while Tori watched them silently.

"My name is John Tucker. I like Tucker better," he said gallantly.

"What's this about White Lightning? Did you try the Rumrunner drink like I did?"

"I don't need a drink. I need to drink you in."

I raised my eyebrows. Grandma got game!

"You look exactly like him. How marvellous." She stretched her wrinkled hand up toward his cheek. He leaned back. She was short enough that she settled for patting him on the shoulder.

"Is White Lightning a *person?*" I couldn't help asking. If so, I'd never heard of him.

She gave a raspy giggle-snort I'd never heard before in an elderly woman. "Oh, dear me. John."

"Tucker, please."

"Tucker. It is my absolute pleasure to call you Tucker."

This time Tori and I exchanged glances.

"Thank you," said Tucker.

"Tucker, my darling, are you telling me that you don't know who White Lightning is?"

"I was today years old when I heard about White Lightning," I said evenly.

Tucker added, in a more kindly tone, "Jennifer told us that it's a white whisky from the southern U.S."

"South Carolina," I reminded him.

"Oh, you poor little dears. It's so droll that you came to Windsor without knowing the local Prohibition history. White Lightning was one of our most famous rumrunners in Windsor."

That was possible. We could look it up later. "And what made you think that Tucker was dressed as him?"

She raised her eyebrows. "Why, the hair, of course. White was world famous for two things: his ability to move alcohol, and his white hair. Whiter than blond."

Tucker smiled. I remembered a study of dementia patients showing that it really upsets them if you correct their facts. It's better if you go along with their delusions. Yes, Grandpa will be here any minute. Yes, I resemble a famous old bootlegger, or in this case, rumrunner.

She jabbed a finger at his hair. "I'd recognize that anywhere."

"It runs in my family," he said. "I get it from my father's side."

"'Course you do. All of us Tuckers turn white before we're thirty." She cackled and pointed at her own white head. "You see?"

Was this woman truly related to my fiancé? I raised my eyebrows and studied her face, searching for a resemblance. Maybe the nose, but it could be the power of suggestion once more.

"I always had blond hair, but you're right, it did turn white before my 25th birthday. My sisters made up a song about it," said Tucker.

What? He'd never mentioned that little nugget. I mean, he'd laughed when I asked him about bleaching his hair, but never volunteered his genetics.

Now that I thought about it, though, his brown eyes were unusual with blond hair, especially in an adult, since towheads often become brunettes with age. It made sense that he actually sported prematurely white hair.

"See? Those are the Tucker genes making their way out of you."

I stifled a laugh. She made it sound like worms. Tori's eyes danced too, catching my meaning.

Tucker didn't care. He took her hand in his, gently. "Your last name is Tucker too? In real life, or for Rogue Con?"

She tutted and reached into her little white purse. It took her a few minutes, but she managed to find her matching wallet and extract her Ontario medical care card.

"Josie Sophia Grant Tucker," I read aloud, comparing the card's crappy photo to her face. It did seem to match.

"Of course it does," she said, as if I'd spoken aloud. "That's the name I was born with."

"Oh, did you choose not to get married, or did you not change your name?" I asked innocently. In the province of Quebec, married women keep their original last names by default, but we were in Ontario now.

"I didn't believe in that shit. I'm a Tucker. Always have, always will be," she shot back.

Whoa. Even though an old lady swore at me, Tucker beamed and said, "When I came to the Rumrunner's Rest, I didn't expect to meet any new relatives! This is off the chain!"

I frowned. Did he actually believe her? Tucker is a common enough name. Try Sze.

"Is that why you messaged me to come meet you?" he continued, in the same cheery voice.

Now I was even more confused.

She covered her mouth, either from surprise or to hide her expression. "My dear Tucker, whatever do you mean?"

"The anonymous message inviting me here." He grinned at her, ignoring my thunderous expression.

What invitation? He'd told me we were here for romance. Since we never got to pre-honeymoon properly in Egypt, we'd try again for a long weekend.

I thought it was weird to invite Tori and her new beau, but some people like to double-date. This was even weirder.

"I can tell you more if you meet me at the ball." Josie all but fluttered her eyelashes at him. Was she seriously flirting with him when they were supposed to be related?

My temples pounded. None of this made sense. I decided to ignore them and check for holes in her story.

I started with the math, with some help from my phone. Americans signed on for a nation-wide Prohibition over a century ago, in 1920; Michigan had started even earlier, in 1917. It lasted until 1933. If I'd pegged her age right, this woman would have been too young to bootleg, and born after it was over. Mmm nope on any first hand rumrunning.

Not that she'd made that claim. But she'd mentioned someone else who had.

To my surprise, I did indeed find a man nicknamed White Lightning during Prohibition. He was famous for both his prematurely white hair and for the airplane he used to fly liquor across the border.

I sat with that for a minute.

Josie Tucker knew what she was talking about, at least enough to cite local Prohibition history.

Was it possible that White Lightning had been a Tucker? And that my fiancé was related to both this woman and a long-dead criminal?

8

EDWIN

Mr. Bagnell's hands tested Edwin's legs next, pinching them hard enough to bruise.

Edwin swallowed. His eyes searched Mrs. Albury's, but she avoided his gaze and smiled at Mr. Bagnell. "Good one, ain't he?"

Mr. Bagnell slapped Edwin's stomach hard enough to make him gasp.

Edwin caught his breath and choked back his tears. Crying would only mean another beating.

Mr. Bagnell grabbed Edwin's hands, studying his nails and twisting the boy's arms back and forth as if to be certain they were attached to his body.

"You afraid of heights?" said Mr. Bagnell.

Edwin blurted out the truth. "No, sir. But I don't like them, sir."

Mr. Bagnell shook him so that Edwin's head bobbed helplessly back and forth. Then the man forced Edwin's mouth open and surveyed his teeth.

Mr. Bagnell stared so long and hard that Edwin worried that his neck would snap. Already, his neck ached and his eyes began to blur.

At last, the terrible pressure released as the man's arm fell away, and Edwin fell with it. He managed to catch himself hard on his palms before his head made contact with the cold floor.

Edwin heard both adults talking above him, although his head continued to whirl, his skin chilled by the floor.

"You said he'd be no trouble," said Mr. Bagnell.

"Oh, no trouble at all, eh, Edwin!" said Mrs. Albury in that strange voice.

"Can't afford another useless one," said Mr. Bagnell.

Mrs. Albury clapped her hands. The sound rang through the parlour. "Not at all, Mr. Bagnell. I can meet you out front with his things straightaway. Off you go, Edwin, there's a good boy."

Edwin forced himself onto his knees. His voice rasped, but he had to speak. "Me nan."

"Shut yer mouth," said Mrs. Albury, but Edwin couldn't stop the words pouring off of his tongue.

"How will me nan find me if I'm gone?"

Mr. Bagnell stared at him with such cold distaste that Edwin trembled and bit his lip while his heart threatened to beat its way out of his chest.

At last, Mr. Bagnell turned to Mrs. Albury. "This one talks too much. Get me the other one."

Edwin's shoulders sagged in relief, but Mrs. Albury's hands fluttered toward the man. "Mr. Bagnell, please. Edwin will make an excellent climbing boy. Edwin, if your nan comes to the orphanage, I'll tell her you're cleaning chimneys with Mr. Bagnell all over Derby. She'll be right proud of you."

Edwin didn't dare speak. He pressed his palms against the floor planks he'd cleaned so many times, scrubbing them with a wire brush and sand. They bleached the floor with lye once a week.

He hadn't realized how lucky he'd been.

Dear Heavenly Father, I promise that if you keep me here, I won't complain, not ever, not even if the lye burns my eyes—

Mr. Bagnell kicked at his chest.

Edwin yelped with pain, even though he twisted to avoid the worst of the blow.

Worse still, Mr. Bagnell's words rained down on him:

"All right, I'll take him."

9

HOPE

"Don't be mad, Hope. I'll tell you why I chose this place," said Tucker right after we closed our hotel room door.

I stared at him. "Does it have to do with the skeleton?" Or Ryan? Averting my eyes from the orange paisley rug that reminded me of amoebas, I chugged some lukewarm water from my stainless steel water bottle.

We'd picked the cheapest room available, so we didn't have our own bathroom, only a wooden double bed that fit under the sloped roof plus a small bedside table holding a clock radio and a glowing ostrich egg-shaped lamp.

"No, of course not." Tucker stood closer to the door, by the mirrored dresser and a tiny wardrobe. "Okay. There's no easy way to tell you. Does this sound familiar?" He straightened his shoulders, threw his head back, and intoned, "'Once in the racket you're always in it.'"

"The racket." I frowned. "That's old-fashioned slang for something. Sounds familiar, but ... maybe something about gambling?"

Tucker sighed, adjusted his face, and tried again. "'When I sell liquor, it's called bootlegging; when my patrons serve it on Lake Shore Drive, it's called hospitality.'"

"He or she says bootlegger, but there has to be a lake if you have a Lake Shore Drive. Hmm." I pondered. "So it's bootlegger from a city with a lake, but we're right around the Great Lakes. Could I get another clue?"

"'The country wanted booze and I organized it. Why should I be called a public enemy?'"

"Okay, we're talking a national scale here. So he's either a big time bootlegger, or someone deluded enough to think he is. I'm assuming it's a he."

Tucker blinked, which I took as a yes.

"And someone in the mob."

"Bing bing bing bing!" Tucker practically made jazz hands in excitement.

I laughed. "Okay. A mob guy who did bootlegging. Didn't they all do it? Do I get one more clue?"

Tucker winked at me. "'Every time a boy falls off a tricycle, every time a black cat has gray kittens, every time someone stubs a toe, every time there's a murder or a fire or the marines land in Nicaragua, the police and the newspapers holler 'Get Capone!'"

"Oh. Al Capone."

Tucker hid his head in his hands. "And they call you the detective doctor."

"I ask them not to." I surveyed him up and down. "So that's why you brought a suit?"

He nodded. "I'm a flipper and I know my onions. Did you know that a flapper was a girl and a flipper was a guy?"

"Clearly not. And knowing your onions means that you're well-versed in Prohibition memes?"

"Pretty much." He unzipped his luggage and soon slicked his hair back with something that looked like grease instead of his usual hair gel. He caught me looking as he wiped his hands. "This was the look. Brilliantine cream. If you couldn't afford it, you used petroleum jelly."

"Yummy."

"To really get it right, I should cut it short on the sides."

"It's already short on the sides."

"Shorter. But I'm not that dedicated." He opened a box in his suitcase.

"A hat?" He'd never worn anything more than a baseball cap. This one was more like a full on fedora.

"To suit the era. But you know."

"Yes, I know." Tucker loves his hair almost as much as he loves me. Which is basically like life itself. "So what does Al Capone have to do with the Rumrunner's Rest? Capone is dead." The Mafia don't interest me, but if Capone was running booze during Prohibition, he'd be over 100 years old now. Even over 120.

"Someone from Rogue Con messaged me on Instagram."

I stared at his phone's message from @no_bull_1920_: a photo of a balding guy with heavy eyebrows and an oversized nose, ears, and lips, but a genuine smile. I couldn't understand his joy, since a sign on his shoulder said U.S. PENITENTIARY ALCATRAZ 85.

Tucker nodded and dropped the hat on his shiny hair. "Capone's mug shot."

I snorted at the message that went with it: *Find him at the Rumrunner's Rest.* "Well, that could be an ad for this hotel. I doubt he's connected to this place, but advertising always bends the rules."

"Keep going."

I paged down the messages. *"'When the lightning struck, the whole prairie would be bathed for a second in white light.'"*

"I looked it up. It's a quote from Larry McMurtry's novel, *Lonesome Dove*."

"I wondered why you'd gotten into Westerns."

"I liked it. I read it because I thought I'd find another clue. But now that we're here ... "

I sighed and sat on the bed, which bowed under my weight. Soft mattress. "It sounds like the key words are lightning and white, right? But why didn't you tell me?"

He shrugged and sank beside me, dropping both of us closer to the floor. "I wanted to surprise you. I didn't tell Tori, either."

"I gathered that."

He nuzzled the skin behind my ear in a way I usually love. "And, in another more honest way, I guess that part of me wants my own adventure. I'm sick of being an also-ran."

"No way." I smiled at him and tugged the hat further down his forehead. "You have that fan site on Instagram."

He smiled a little. "It has a few hundred followers."

"Mine's non-existent."

"Before Kevin pulled yours, you had 49K."

I waved my hands in dismissal, although it bothered me that he knew my former followers to the thousand. "Your TikTok will get there. And do you seriously want what I have?"

"I know you hate it. And I wish I didn't care." The tendons in his neck bulged. "But I'm a media whore. I wish they'd pay attention to me."

"Stalker and all?"

"Nah. I'd take the offers for photo shoots and free swag—"

"Free vegan makeup and meal kits? You can have mine."

He sighed. "It embarrasses the hell out of me, Hope. Trust me. I'm trying to get over it. But in the meantime, I kind of wanted this."

"Okay." I got that. Well, not really. Ryan resented playing second fiddle to my medical career. Tucker matched my career, but I outranked him as an amateur sleuth. Seemed like I couldn't help hurting ye olde male ego, even in the 21st century. "So you got these weird messages, and as soon as we arrived, they found a skeleton."

"And Rogue Con moved its ball here after a fire. It all seems planned," said Tucker.

"Huge coincidence otherwise," I agreed. But did that mean Marina and Ryan were in on it? I couldn't imagine Ryan playing along. "The fire is ominous."

Tucker's face lit up. "I heard it was because someone was trying to heat up a pocket p—um, a sex aid with a hairdryer and started a really minor fire. The hotel's okay."

"Are you serious?"

"Yup."

I cackled. "Okay. But do you have any idea why someone would set all of this up for you?"

Chapter 9

He pulled his fedora down on his forehead and hooked his one visible eyebrow at me. "It's a puzzle they want me to solve."

"Right, but how would that help them? Did they even plan the bones in the fireplace?"

Tucker laughed. "I don't think this would go back to 1920."

"Right. So they figured out the bones were here. What made them say, let's get Tucker here and uncover them? What's the benefit to the organizer?"

He pondered that for a minute before he shrugged. "I don't know. It's pretty awesome, though, right?"

"I don't think human remains in chimneys are awesome."

"You know what I mean."

"Nope." I'd rather save lives at the hospital, then live out a peaceful life with my man, two kids, and a dog like Roxy, Ryan's foster Rottweiler.

Tucker's expression closed down. "You think it's for you."

"Huh? I didn't say that."

"But you think it, right? If someone's luring the Great Brain, they mean you. Not me. But I'm the one they want to talk to."

Frankly, if a stranger named @no_bull_1920_ had messaged me about Al Capone and the Rumrunner's Rest, not only would I block @no_bull_1920_, I'd add them to my crazy pile.

(I do have a crazy pile. Kevin reads all the messages. He claims that it doesn't bother him, and that he's more organized and more motivated than our parents. Can't argue with that one. Our parents still have a hard time grasping that I'm an M.D. who can buy her own milk, let alone the whole sleuth sideline.)

So yeah. I did think someone had planted a trap. Someone who knew Tucker well enough to appeal to his ego and to his curiosity.

Unfortunately, that doesn't narrow down the suspects. Tucker has two sisters, umpteen cousins, and makes new friends approximately every 2.2 seconds. He also might be slightly toasted right now.

That meant that I'd have to stay alert for both of us. I unzipped my suitcase and tossed my underwear and bras in the upper drawer of the dresser.

Since Ryan was here, any potential organizer also knew *me* well enough to distract me with the best weapon possible: another man I still loved and could no longer have, while I still loved the man I was with.

One of my socks bounced on the ground. As I scooped it up, my eye fell on the wall socket, which looked suspiciously loose.

10

MARCH 29, BRIGGS BREWERY

EDWIN

Mr. Bagnell shoved open the front door of the brick building. "Right. Go on."

Edwin eyed the smoke rising from the brewhouse's narrow chimney before he clutched the sacking on his shoulder and silently followed Mr. Bagnell into the room that smelled like sweat and beer.

Almost immediately, Edwin felt the room's warmth seep into his skin. He lived barefoot and slept huddled with the other boys under the sacks they used to catch the soot during the day.

"Eh. They left the fire on," said Mr. Bagnell.

Edwin stared at the orange flames leaping from the coal held by the metal grate, which acted as a basket of metal to keep the coal off the hearth. A single shard of coal burned through the grate and fell on the hearth with a near-soundless thump.

Edwin bit back a whimper.

His knees and elbows smarted. The other boys said he'd learn how to climb with them. They said it was a good thing Mr. Bagnell had toughened them up by holding him by the hot fire and rubbing brine into his skin with a brush while Edwin screamed. But Edwin thought he'd never get used to the pain, or the soot that stung his eyes, or the daily dread of wedging himself into chimneys.

Today, fire was his first enemy.

"I told you to put that out," Mr. Bagnell called to the owner of the brewpub.

The owner retorted, "Bugger that! I got customers here."

Three customers glanced up from their mugs before they turned back to their beer.

"Can't go up a chimney with a fire in it." Mr. Bagnell crossed his arms. "That's a death warrant, it is."

Edwin's heart leapt. For once, he would get away. They would come back and do the brewhouse another day. That chimney frightened him. He could hardly look at it.

The owner muttered and grumbled before he doused the fire with a pot of water.

The fire hissed like a furious cat as it died. Steam and smoke wafted into the chimney flue and spread partway into the room, causing the men to cough as the owner used a poker to drag the grate out of the hearth.

Mr. Bagnell shoved his brush at Edwin, who gulped as he accepted it. Mr. Bagnell couldn't mean that he should climb up the steaming chimney straightaway.

"Go on, then." Mr. Bagnell's voice lowered dangerously.

11

HOPE

Tucker's shadow fell over me. "What's wrong, Hope?"

I knelt beside the wall socket, using a pair of chopsticks to pull it away from the wall. Or trying to. "I can see something. They didn't even screw the plate back in properly. Good thing I found some chopsticks in my bag."

"You're supposed to turn off the circuit if you fool around with electricity."

"I know, but I can't ask Jennifer to shut off the electricity for the whole Rumrunner's Rest because the wall socket was loose."

He reached for the chopsticks. "Look. If you're really worried about it, call the front desk and ask for maintenance. This is insane."

Someone knocked on our door, surprising both of us. Tucker stood up, and I jerked the chopsticks, revealing the thing in the hole behind the wall socket before I fell on my butt.

Tucker peered through our door's peephole while I turned on my phone light to eyeball the newly-revealed hole in our room.

"Oh, hey guys," said Tucker, opening the door.

So it wasn't Ryan.

I closed my eyes and cursed myself. It was too light a knock for

Ryan, and he was probably worshipping his new girlfriend's big, beautiful bosom right now.

Okay, that sounded wrong.

"What are you doing, Hope?" Tori knelt beside me. She was wearing ... blackface? No, she'd smeared blacking on her forehead and cheeks but left the area around her eyes and nose clear. She also wore all black, from a baseball cap to her sandals.

Griffin wore a similar outfit, but had only blacked under his eyes like a football player.

"You know it's not cool to wear blackface anymore, right?" Tucker asked her.

Griffin snorted. "It's not blackface. It's more like an occupational hazard. You gonna tell 'em?"

"Tell us what?" I asked.

Tori exhaled and closed her eyes before shaking her head.

I stood up, temporarily distracted from the wall socket hole. "Seriously, Tori. Does this have something to do with your ... mystical figure?" At the last minute, I remembered not to say *ghost* in case she hadn't told Griffin. I'm classy like that.

"I'm not up to it right now, Hope. I'll tell you soon, I promise." She stared at me and my chopsticks. "What are you doing?"

"I looked behind, um ... " My voice died out when I realized that maybe someone was spying on us, based on whatever I'd found behind the wall socket. So instead of talking, I held up my phone light to illuminate the hidey hole.

Griffin gave a low whistle. Tori grabbed my arm and backed me away from the little green plastic circuit board with wires hanging from it. Tucker switched on his own phone light and studied it before he took pictures and texted them to me and Tori.

Griffin wrote on his phone's notes, then held it up for all of us to read: **that's a circuit board**

And a microphone, Tori added.

My eyes widened. Yes, my father kept a few of these circuit boards at home, now that they mentioned it. He and Kevin used them for programming.

Chapter 11

Tori tapped on her phone and showed me a picture of what looked like a little metal bullet, but turned out to be a self-described "LDC Condenser Microphone."

I sucked in my breath and started to speak before I remembered to type it on my phone instead. **Do you see a camera?**

They studied their pictures and the hole, then one by one, they shook their heads.

Griffin searched the hole a bit more and used the chopsticks to withdraw a folded piece of paper. At a glance, it appeared to be a copy of an old newspaper interview with White Lightning, which was cool but not immediately relevant.

This is whacked, I wrote. **We need a new room.**

Tori responded first after showing her message to Griffin, who nodded. **You can switch rooms with us.**

I shook my head. **I'm afraid it's my stalker.**

then it's ok. he doesn't want us, typed Griffin.

At the back of my mind, I was impressed that he used good apostrophes, if not capitalization. Tori had chosen wisely. But I said, **No. Maybe he'd switch over to you and Tori. It's not safe.**

It could be my messenger. Tucker smiled.

I stared at him in disbelief. **We need to get out of here.** I quickly texted the circuit board picture to my parents, Kevin, and, even though he'd blocked me, Ryan the engineer.

Tucker tapped out, **You can try to get a new room, but everywhere is pretty booked up because of Rogue Con. Let's talk to Jennifer.**

I glared at Tucker. He wanted to solve this more than he cared about our privacy. **Jennifer could be in on it.**

Tori waved to get our attention and showed us her phone. **Take our room while you figure something out.**

Tucker raised his eyebrows. He thought I was overreacting. 'Cause *he* wasn't the one with the stalker.

I didn't want to endanger Tori, but I had to get away from that microphone.

We packed up our stuff and switched rooms as quietly as possible.

Then we walked downstairs, past what Tucker said was the honeymoon suite. He pointed at the door. "We could level up, Hope. That was the only free room, last I checked."

I quickly loaded the Rumrunner's Rest website up on my phone. "Sold out."

He grinned and waggled his eyebrows at me. "Too bad. We could've used the hot tub next door."

"Maybe later," said Tori, quelling the innuendo as we moved outside through the side door, toward the parking lot.

I'd forgotten my rain gear, but Tori had brought an umbrella that she tried to hold over me, Griffin, and herself. Not so easy with the height discrepancy between us and her man.

The parking lot was surprisingly full. Only two disabled spaces and the spot for electric cars were unclaimed. Tucker paused beside his old black Toyota, letting the rain soak his hair. "Want to go for a ride instead?"

I patted my jeans pocket. I still had our car keys on me, but I shook my head. "I want to stay close to the WiFi so I can look for hotel rooms without burning my data."

"Fair," said Tucker. "I want to do a bit of research myself on the Rumrunner's Rest."

"That's easy," said Tori. I tried not to laugh at her mouth moving in the middle of her black makeup, against the backdrop of the rain. "Like Javier said, the Dreamland Inn was built in 1920." Griffin held the umbrella so she could text us both the website link.

When I glanced up from the oversold hotel listings, Tucker read aloud, "'The Dreamland Inn was renovated in 1925, with all restorations complete by 1928.'"

That basement looked like it hadn't been renovated since, but to be fair, how many tourists checked out the basement?

"So the skeleton couldn't be older than 1920, or 1928 if the renovations included blocking off the chimney," said Griffin.

Thunder rumbled in the distance. I glanced uneasily at the sky over the lake. "Unless someone kept an old set of bones and dumped them down the chimney some years later," I said.

Chapter 11

Griffin hiked one eyebrow at me while Tori placed a blackened hand on his arm. "Hope has seen a lot of strange things."

"I'm also mad that everything's booked from Airbnb to hotels. I can't find anything starting under $390 a night. In Windsor!"

"It's Rogue Con," said Tucker. "I'm surprised anything's available at all."

I changed the subject. "Anyway, I agree with Griffin. Chances are, those bones made their way here about 100 years ago, assuming that nobody imported them. That narrows down the *when* part. And the chimney is the *where*. But as one of my journalist friends pointed out, we need to know *who, what,* and *how.*"

I pulled out my phone and typed
WHEN: 1920-now
WHERE: chimney
WHO
WHAT
HOW

The wind shifted and blew fine raindrops at my phone. I swiftly pocketed it. I can't afford another one.

"By *who*, you mean who do the bones belong to? Or who put them there?" Tucker tilted his head as he considered. His hat stayed in place.

"Both," Tori and I said together.

"The coroner and the forensic anthropologist will be able to tell us more," I said.

"Yeah, but not on a Friday night, and maybe not for months to come," said Tucker. "Plus they probably won't tell us anything beyond a media release."

"I wonder if anyone else here could let us in on a secret." I eyeballed Tori and Griffin. Under the umbrella, that's uncomfortably close.

Tori flushed, avoiding my gaze.

"Why do you think we'd know anything?" Griffin met me straight on, daring me to ask.

"I don't know. But are you supposed to be covered in soot? As in, from a chimney?" I asked him right back.

Their gazes met before Tori gave a tiny nod. Griffin sighed and let go of Tori, spreading his big hands in front of him. "Yeah."

Tucker whistled a song I recognized, "With a Little Bit of Luck," squinting in the rain.

Tori gave a scant laugh. "Wrong show, Tucker. That's from 'My Fair Lady.'"

"My bad." Tucker started dancing, knees up, elbows out, and somehow I recognized it from the rooftop scene in Mary Poppins.

Tori looked stricken. Griffin drew her into his chest and murmured in her ear until she nodded and drew a deep breath. "You both got me. Yes. I was dreaming about chimneys even before tonight."

Wordlessly, I gestured at the hotel so she could rest. She shook her head. "I don't want to dream anymore. I think it would be worse here. More vivid."

Griffin cleared his throat. "She talks about 'climbing boys' in her sleep."

I'd never heard that term before, but I could guess.

Griffin nodded. "They used to force kids to sweep chimneys. They'd take orphans—"

"Or parents would sell them because they couldn't afford to feed them anymore," Tori quietly interjected.

I gulped. That still happens today. In rich countries too. There are always hungry children and desperate or indifferent parents.

"I read up on it to try and understand the history," said Tori. "After the Great Fire in London in 1666 burned down four fifths of London, they started regulating chimneys and the need to keep them clean. That's when they turned to climbing boys, who could fit into tiny spaces."

"It was sick," said Griffin. "I read about it, how they used six-year-olds—"

Tori nodded. "Even as young as four. Mostly boys, but girls too.

Chapter 11

They were so little that their bones became deformed, especially their knees and ankles, since they usually had to shimmy up the flue—the insides of the chimney—using their back, knees, elbows, and ankles. They'd be stuck in odd positions. They'd brush out the soot with one hand. The soot would fall on them, irritating their lungs and inflaming their eyes. They had to break off creosote with their other hand. Then they'd have to scoop out the soot fallen in the hearth for their master to sell."

I stared at her, imagining her as a child, crawling those chimneys with tearless determination.

"They died all the time," said Griffin.

"Chimney Sweep Cancer." Tucker knotted his hands, blanching the knuckles.

I raised my eyebrows. I know Tucker's the master of all things odd, and could win Trivial Pursuit any day, but how'd he know that?

"Yes, that was their name for scrotal cancer, which killed them as teenagers because of their exposure to carcinogens. It was very painful." Tori gazed from me to Tucker. "But some died even sooner. They were trapped and asphyxiated inside the flues. You had to climb in a certain way, with your knees below your waist, or you'd get stuck."

Tucker walked away from us. Griffin took over, raising his voice.

"Yeah, you could climb the wrong way and get lost. If you got stuck, they might throw a rope down from the top to pull you out, or send another boy up after you to tie a rope around your ankle and drag you out the bottom. Once two climbing boys died that way because they both got stuck."

I could see why Tori was haunted, figuratively and maybe literally, by these terrible stories. I cleared my throat.

She continued, "People tried to save money by not calling for a climbing boy until a dangerous amount of soot had built up. The child might suffocate under its weight. Sometimes the chimney was already on fire, and the master would force a child up, then throw a bucket of water on them from the top."

"Stop," said Tucker. Strangely, he held his palms up at us in a "no more" gesture, trying to smile but looking all the more ghastly for it. "I think I might—"

He opened the door and hurried back inside the Rumrunner's Rest, slamming the wooden door behind him.

12

I've never seen Tucker say no.

I've never seen him say stop.

He always wants more. More sex, in different positions, anytime, anywhere. More music—have you heard this song? It's epic. It's fire.

More languages. More medicine. More beer.

This time, he fled. I lingered outside the public bathroom to the left of the stairs. "Tucker?"

He gagged in answer.

I hurried further down the hall, shaking my head. If this were a sitcom, he'd be pregnant.

"Is he okay?" asked Tori, her eyes shadowed as she followed me.

"He's nauseated," I said. In medical school, a lecturer once gave us a speech about the difference between nauseous and nauseated.

"Brutal," said Griffin.

"Yeah. Are you okay?" I asked Tori, although I glanced at Griffin to include him.

She shrugged and gazed out the window facing the river. Michigan was so close that the few lights shining through the rain might actually be beaming toward us from Detroit.

Tucker gargled so loud, I could almost taste it. I hurried down the hall.

Tori and Griffin kept pace behind me, holding hands. "Is this the hot tub?" I asked, pointing to the door on our first right.

"No, that's the honeymoon suite," said Griffin, and I noticed the big blue star hanging on the door sported a white tiara on one point and a top hat on another. Pretty heteronormative, like most of the wedding industry.

Light seeped from underneath the door, but I didn't hear anyone inside it. I hurried past anyway.

The next room said HOT TUB and had a long list of rules underneath, like showering before you got in, no alcohol, no breakable glass, etc. I pushed on the door. It was locked, so I used my key card to unlock the door to the small room.

Two bearded men frowned at me from a beige fibreglass hot tub, all jets firing and two ficus trees framing them. A towel rack and bin were discreetly placed behind the trees, against the wooden wall.

"Sorry," I mouthed at them, and let the door fall closed. All guests were allowed to use the hot tub, but I wasn't about to leap in between two guys in my jeans.

Tori and Griffin had retreated back toward the bathroom. I followed them and noted that Tucker had fallen mercifully quiet.

Griffin nodded at me as the toilet flushed. "How was the hot tub?"

"Occupied," I said, trying not to blush. "Maybe we can go later."

"I'm not into that stuff," he said, but Tori said, "Sure."

While Tucker ran the faucet, I said, "About the climbing boys."

Tori nodded, pressing her lips together.

"Is your ghost a climbing boy?" I asked her directly.

After a long moment, she nodded again.

Tori is a woman of few words. Did she literally see the spirit of a little kid covered in coal dust, or did she mean it metaphorically?

I tried to ask in a neutral way, "What do you know about him?"

Griffin slung his arm around her. I noticed how often he touched her, whether because he loved her or he needed to reassure her, or both.

I let go of my suspicion of him. I don't trust people easily. I consider few people good enough for Tori, and I thought it was odd that he wasn't in the basement when Jennifer had led us down. He'd texted Tori to come, but he'd come down the stairs later himself.

Yet he'd offered their room to me and Tucker. And the basement time discrepancy could be as simple as him going to the bathroom on the main floor and then getting stuck in the swarm of Rogue Con. Tucker and Ryan don't slip through crowds the way I do. They let others go first. "If I moved the way you do, someone would punch me," Tucker once told me. I assume that goes double for a tall Black man.

Griffin and Tori really seemed to love each other. Even more impressive since they'd forged their relationship while researching climbing boys, a boner killer if there ever was one (literally. See: scrotal cancer).

While Tucker rattled the paper towel dispenser handle, Tori told the window about her ghost. "He's six. Or he thinks he is. He's not sure."

Six. Prime age for a climbing boy. I exhaled.

"He lives in an orphanage with Mrs. Albury."

"Okay. Do you know his name?"

She sighed. "Edwin." Her voice rose and broke on the first syllable.

"And the name of the orphanage?"

She didn't answer. Griffin checked with her before he took over. "There's no record of him. We think it's the St Elizabeth's Orphanage of Mercy, because that was run by a woman named Albury."

"Where was the St Elizabeth's Orphanage of Mercy?" I asked.

"Derby. It's in England. The East Midlands."

"And when was that operational?"

"Mrs. Albury ran it from 1830 to 1848."

I'm weak on English history, but that was certainly after the Great Fire in 1666, and a quick check on my phone confirmed that climbing boys were a thing in the 1700's and 1800's.

"Do you think Edwin has anything to do with the bones we found in the chimney tonight?" I asked quietly.

"I don't know," Tori told the window.

Different continent. Different century. I'd have to ask Tucker, who'd gotten the closest look at those bones, but a six-year-old would have a much smaller humerus than an adult.

"When did you start researching Edwin?" I kept my voice even.

She passed a hand over her eyes. "I'd say it started the night we booked the trip. I didn't think it was related, but last night I dreamed—"

"What?" I asked, after waiting.

She shook her head.

"She doesn't want to talk about it," said Griffin.

"I got that." I tried to gentle my voice. "I'm not judging you, Tori. My family ... " How to say this. "We've talked about ghosts before. It's not as big a deal to us as other people."

She turned, but her gaze fixed on my forehead. "Have you seen any ghosts?"

I couldn't lie. I shook my head.

She looked at Griffin, who kissed the top of her head and murmured in her ear.

At last, she met my eyes, and hers were so sad that my stomach plunged even before her voice splintered. "I'm not crazy."

13

EDWIN

Edwin had heard of other boys who'd hesitated in the lower chimney, near the hearth, afraid to climb further up. Mr. Bagnell had lit a straw fire under one named George. "That got him moving! He sprang up like a monkey, crying the whole time!"

George's breeches had burned. The remaining charred fabric had stuck to the red, blistered skin of his feet and legs, but he'd kept working that day, and the week after, until he got the chills and refused to rise, no matter how Mr. Bagnell had beaten him.

George had disappeared the next morning. Edwin daren't ask what happened to him.

Edwin edged toward the hearth, squeezing his eyes shut as he prayed. He prayed that his nan would find him. That was what his mother had always said, that no matter what, Nan would come for both of them.

Next Edwin swept the hearth out and spread the sacking to catch the soot. They could sell the soot afterward for 9d a bushel, although he was afraid the cloth would catch fire first from a stray spark.

Mr. Bagnell grunted, "We'll come down from the top, this time."

Edwin sucked in his breath. He'd been granted a tiny reprieve, as long as the chimney temperature dropped in the few minutes he clambered up the slate roof.

Edwin had learned how to climb. Mr. Bagnell claimed that the bare skin of the boys' feet helped them grip the brick better, and Edwin now knew how to clutch with his fingers and search out every toehold. Most of all, he knew that when he descended the chimney, he must not let his knees and hips fold up above his waist and wedge him inside the chimney flue. His own legs could suffocate him. The boys told him that someone named Joseph had died this way.

14

HOPE

Tori and Griffin had left by the time Tucker made his way back to our borrowed room, citing privacy, but I couldn't help dwelling on the sorrow in her eyes.

"I'm that good a host, eh?" Tucker said, trying to laugh as he grabbed his toiletry kit and headed to the upstairs bathroom we shared with Tori, Griffin, and another room.

"Awesome host," I called to his back, since that was a point of pride for him. He waved as the door shut behind him.

No one wanted to talk to me.

I checked for hidden microphones. The whole room looked similar to our previous one, except this one had blue accessories instead of orange, and more importantly, no obvious spyware. I plopped on the bed, which was slightly firmer than the other one, and made notes on my phone.

What had happened to the person in the chimney?

Who had invited Tucker to the Rumrunner's Rest? Was Al Capone actually involved?

Did Josie Tucker know anything besides the name of a long-ago bootlegger? Was she truly related to my fiancé?

Was it a coincidence that Ryan had shown up after months of blocking me?

I left Tori for last. Her story worried me.

I twisted my fingers through my hair, which I'd started growing out to shoulder length again, and bolded the first two questions. I was most worried about the person in the chimney and Tucker's invitation. The rest could wait. As long as Tori was okay. Otherwise, I'd bump her up to number one. Love her.

The chimney bothered me because it was a trap. It had literally been a trap for whoever had died there. Even if the bones had been thrown in as an afterthought, that was still not what you'd call resting in peace.

I started researching the Rumrunner's Rest, using the hotel's pretty good WiFi, when the hotel phone rang. I picked up the extension, bracing myself for more bad news.

"Hi, is this Dr. Hope Sze?" The woman's voice was pitched low, young but self-assured.

"Yes." I frowned, trying to place the voice.

"This is Jennifer. I wanted to thank you and Dr. Tucker for your help this afternoon and apologize for your room. Dr. Yamamoto told me that there was something in the wall socket. I sent a man in to check that out."

Oh, Jennifer the bartender. It seemed a bit unusual for her to call instead of the owner or manager, but maybe the Rumrunner's Rest had a small staff. "Yes, we were concerned. It looked like a microphone and a circuit board. Dr. Yamamoto called you about it?"

"No, I was looking for you and Dr. Tucker, and she answered the phone in room 12. I want to assure you that we've never had a problem like this before. Never. We take privacy seriously at the Rumrunner's Rest."

"I see."

"As you can imagine, trust was everything in the days of Prohibition, and we uphold that trust to this day."

Right. Trust among thieves. "We were happy to help out with the discovery. Did you hear back from the forensic anthropologist

Chapter 14

already?" Seemed unlikely, but it felt like anything could happen here.

"I'm afraid not. I wanted to thank you and ask if there was anything I could do to make your stay more comfortable."

Wow. This was the equivalent of upgrading your next flight if you gave medical help on an airplane. "I can't think of anything. Unless you can make sure that Dr. Yamamoto feels all right?" I winced at myself. Tori was so intensely private, but she worried me.

"I've already taken care of your drinks as well as those for Dr. Yamamoto and Mr. Chao, of course."

"Of course," I murmured to myself, noting two things. Griffin was definitely part Chinese with a name like that. Cool. On the other hand, it didn't look like the Rumrunner's Rest was grateful enough to comp either of our rooms, despite the spy equipment. "I'm trying to find out more about White Lightning and the history of the Rumrunner's Rest, if you have any references about that."

I could hear the smile in her voice. "Ah, you want to hear about Miss Gertrud."

"Gertrud?"

"Gertrud Adams, the owner of the Dreamland Inn. Gertrud was a tall, beautiful, buxom woman born in Germany. She married a man in Chicago, moved to Windsor as a widow, and became a pioneer of the roadhouse business."

I blinked. "That's quite an accomplishment."

"She was legendary. She built Dreamland herself and fought for every penny."

"I wonder how she was able to secure a loan in 1925," I said. "It couldn't have been easy for a woman." Let alone a widow—no man to secure it—and there must've been some anti-German sentiment post-World War I.

"She bootstrapped it, as far as I understand. She bought the restaurant when it was a little three-room building. She was the cook and the waitress because she couldn't afford to hire anyone else. She served the best 'shore dinners.' This was the most famous and the most popular establishment all around. And she renovated it all by 1928. Did you notice the gingerbread entrances?"

"Gingerbread?"

She laughed. "The decorative wooden pieces at the front. The walls in the honeymoons suite are made of mahogany. Nothing but the best for Mrs. Adams. She made wonderful perch dinners and hired the best bands."

I tried to guess the genre. "Jazz bands?"

"Of course. That was the revolutionary music of its time. Did you know that Ella Fitzgerald played at the Elmwood Casino Hotel here in Windsor? That was in 1971, though, long after Gertrud disappeared."

I gripped the plastic receiver. "Excuse me?"

"Gertrud Adams vanished in 1946. We never figured out what happened to her. Of course it wasn't easy to keep Dreamland running after Prohibition ended, and some people thought she might have been kidnapped, or have run away, but no one knew what happened."

"What about the skeleton we found in the chimney tonight?" Was it Gertrud? The long-ago owner whom they thought had taken off, but in fact had never left her own building?

I rubbed my forehead. Tucker slipped back in the room and raised his eyebrows at me as he closed the door behind himself, but I shook my head. How on earth could you solve a murder when you didn't even know who had died?

Jennifer was already answering me. "Yes, I thought of her when we found the bones."

"Did you tell the police?"

Tucker stopped zipping up his Dopp kit on the dresser. He crossed the room to sit on the bed with me, listening intently. I tilted the phone receiver so he could hear better.

"I mentioned it," said Jennifer. "They already knew. Gertrud is a legend. We had school trips out here. It's part of local history."

"Let's go on the assumption that it was Gertrud." It was possible that the butler did it—if she had a butler—but I'd bet on someone else with close proximity. "Did she have a boyfriend or second husband who would have harmed her?"

"Not that we know of. They say that Gertrud was kind of secretive and probably a workaholic. My mom talked to one of the waitresses who used to work here—"

I brightened, even though it seemed far-fetched. "She's still alive?"

"Oh, no. She was only 16 when she worked here, but she passed away years ago. She was friends with my grandmother, who took care of her, and that's how I got interested in history, especially Prohibition."

"And how you started working here," I surmised.

"Sort of. Is there anything else I can help you with?"

"Do you know White Lightning too?"

Tucker gave me the thumbs up.

She sighed. "I know that he disappeared in 1928."

15

Tucker jerked straight up in shock.

I stared at the phone in my hand. "You said that *Gertrud* disappeared."

"She did. In 1946."

"And White Lightning, the most famous bootlegger in the area—"

"Also vanished, but much sooner than her."

"In 1928."

"You remembered!" Jennifer sounded pleased.

"Yeah, I haven't lost my short term memory yet. How come no one mentioned that the Rumrunner's Rest is like the Bermuda Triangle for swallowing people up?"

She chuckled. "I wouldn't say that. It was the Dreamland Inn at first. After Gertrud ... left, it was abandoned and claimed by the city. An entrepreneur reopened the restaurant, which only lasted a few years. The city wanted to make it into a retirement home. But Gilbert and Sherry Gervais bought it in 1980 and built it up to the success it is today."

"That's interesting." Either the hotel website had glossed over the years of unsuccessful businesses, or my friends hadn't bothered mentioning it to me.

"As for Gertrud Adams and White Lightning, I wouldn't assume the worst. People moved around. You can imagine that during Prohibition, and afterwards, during World War II, the population changed from one day to the next."

"Right." Rumrunners and Prohibition officers moved in and out of the city, men signed up as soldiers, women worked in factories, and veterans might make it home or start a new life elsewhere. I could imagine the chaos of trying to rebuild after the Second World War. A woman could easily go missing. It must have been traumatic to survive not one World War, but two. "So do you think it could be Gertrud or White Lightning's bones we found in the chimney?"

"Oh, I wouldn't know. I'll leave that to you."

"Thanks, Jennifer. See you at the ball." Before she hung up, I overheard her say, "Do you need help with your cart, sir?"

Tucker bounced off the bed and grabbed his cell phone before I hung up the landline receiver. "I gotta know more about White Lightning."

"Hang on. What happened to you when Tori was talking about Edwin?"

He turned away from me and marched back to the window. "Nothing. I'm good now."

"You started to throw up. Too much alcohol?"

That made him crack a smile. "What? I barely had anything. I'm not like you."

He teased me about my minimal liquor tolerance, but I remembered how avidly he'd finished my Bearcat, and couldn't fake a smile back. "Seriously. You started to lose it with the talk about climbing boys. Did you need a trigger warning? I know it's not easy—"

"That's not it," Tucker insisted, even though he still looked pale around the eyes and mouth. "Maybe I ate or drank something off. I'm okay now. We've got 45 minutes before the ball. Let's dig up all we can on White Lightning and Gertrud Adams."

"You already dressed?" I eyed him up and down. He'd cleaned up well. I didn't detect any wet spots, let alone vomit.

"Everything except my tie clip. I got a special one that was passed down through my dad's family. I haven't decided if I'm going to wear it or not." A shadow flickered across his face.

"Can I see it?"

He unlocked his suitcase. I hid a frown as he turned the little key and tucked the key back in his suit pocket. Normally Tucker doesn't lock his luggage.

He opened a small, black velvet case and showed me the tie clip. I held my breath for a second.

The silver clip looked almost like a hair barrette, except for the fine engraving along its length. However, that only served as a backdrop to the figure on the front.

The black octagon held a female figure kicking her feet up behind her. She raised her arms in the air, palms up to the sky. She held her left arm higher than the right, and a series of lines radiated out from her left hand, the way I'd make a sun "shine" when I was drawing with crayons.

"It's beautiful," I said quietly. I'm not into flashy jewels, but this tie clip radiated a kind of dignity and power.

"My father gave it to me the day I graduated from medical school. It's a family heirloom. I don't use it much. You can see it's already damaged."

I could. The figure's left leg, from the knee down, had ... fallen out? Gotten chipped?

"I brought it for the closing ball. My dad would kill me if I lost or wrecked it."

I cleared my throat and asked the key question. "Where did it come from?"

"An Uncle Fred passed it down through the generations." He grinned at me. "I'm supposed to give it to my son."

I squeezed his arm. There's no guarantee we'll be lucky enough to have a son, but still. "You going to wear it tonight?"

"I don't know. I don't want to lose it, and no one would even notice it at Rogue Con."

"Josie Tucker would," I said.

"Yeah. I thought of that." He hesitated and closed the box lid.

"Anyway. You ready to change?" He set the tie clip box on our bedside table, beside the clock radio, and we both stared at it before he quickly locked her back in his suitcase.

"I want to keep her safe. I know I'm being superstitious," he said, before drawing me back onto the bed.

"No problem," I said as he extended my arms above my head and started pulling off my shirt. "I don't want her to watch."

16

My phone buzzed and woke me up. Somehow, I'd managed to nod off.

It took me a split second to blink my dried-out contact lenses back into place and read the message from Kevin's new phone.

Hope! We're coming.

Me: *No, I'm not in Montreal. I'm in Windsor. We're on vacation.*

Kevin: *I know!* 🔥

Me: *Are you really on your way to Windsor?*

Kevin: 🕶️👋🚗

What? I tried calling. Kevin didn't pick up. Maybe they'd hit a patch of bad reception while Dad drove. I waited a minute for them to hit another cell tower, and then I tried my mom instead.

"Oh, hello?" she said, with a faintly pleased air.

"Mom. It's me."

"Yes, hello! Sorry, I can't hear you. We're driving."

I enunciated my words carefully over the hum of their tires on the road, which even I could hear. "Mom. Are you driving towards me?"

"What's that? Yes!"

"You're coming here? How do you know where I am?"

"Win! The Rumrunner's Rest!"

I stared at my own phone in disbelief. My friends occasionally said "Win!" after something good, but not my mom. Maybe she'd picked it up from Kevin. I had a more important question, though. "Mom, I didn't tell you where we were staying. Tucker wanted to surprise me. How did you—"

"What's that? I can't hear you. He gave me a new phone, but I don't know how to use it yet. Maybe he'll teach me tonight."

"What? Dad gave you a new phone? And Kevin too?"

"Of course not!"

I rolled my eyes. Sometimes I give up. "Mom, give me to Kevin. And tell Dad to be careful driving. Remember my case where a toddler died from a car's power window—"

"What's that?"

"Mom! I want to talk to Kevin!"

"Huh?"

"Kevin!"

"Yes, Kevin's here. Sorry, love, I can't hear you. We'll see you soon." She hung up.

What the helllllllllll.

Tucker stirred, keeping his bare arm and leg still draped over me. He kissed my cheek. "The whole Sze clan is coming?"

"I guess so. My mom said the Rumrunner's Rest. I can't imagine there's more than one of those."

"Are they coming to Rogue Con?"

"I have no idea. My brother texted something about Mr. Ng, but maybe that was spellcheck." My phone felt warm, almost hot, in my hand.

Me: *Who is Mr. Ng? Did he tell you to come? Remember the celery.*

Celery has a stalk. Like my unknown stalker. Kevin and I sometimes talked about him in code, partly so as not to worry my parents, and partly because the stalker was less scary if we could make fun of him.

I'm paranoid, but seriously, how could they know my location if *I* hadn't known where Tucker had booked and I hadn't had a chance to tell them? I kissed the most obvious answer to wake him back up. "Did you tell them we were going to the Rumrunner's Rest, before you told me?"

He chuckled and partly rolled back on top of me. "No way. It's supposed to be our getaway, remember?"

I did my best to shrug underneath him. "So, Tori or Griffin?"

"I guess it's possible."

"Unlikely." Why would Tori, let alone near-stranger Griffin, invite my entire family to join us?

And Ryan had showed up with his titty girlfriend, we'd found bones in the RR's fireplace, plus Tori seemed at least figuratively and maybe literally haunted.

"This is messed up," I said aloud.

Tucker laughed and reached for his hat, which he'd stuck on a bed post. "We'll see 'em if we Sze 'em. I guess your family can't get enough of me."

Tucker's always in a good mood after sex. I swatted his rear end. He was still naked except for the hat.

He picked his watch off of his miniature wooden bedside table. "We better go to the ball."

"Just a second. I want to read up first."

"About White Lightning?"

"And Gertrud Adams." Both of them had been alive and kicking during Prohibition, and both of them had suddenly disappeared. It didn't guarantee that one or both of them had ended up in the chimney, but I had my suspicions.

"Let me start with the newspaper article that was in the hole," I said. Griffin and Tori had each taken photos of it on their phones and then left us the original, which was on plain white paper, not yellowed and tattered like a hundred-year-old real original.

The article's opening explained that White Lightning was a bootlegger who wished to remain anonymous. I glanced at the black and white photo that showed his white hair, shadowed face, and spiffy suit. I skipped on to the actual interview where the man started to talk, interspersed with questions from the interviewer.

How did you start in the rumrunning business?

My brother worked at the Rainbow Inn. He gave me twenty dollars a week to help him serve beer and clean up. Wasn't much, but I could eat and sleep there.

That twenty dollars came in handy because I'd head down to the dock—

Which dock?

I'm not giving you the address. Our dock. Our other brother owns it. It's part of our farm that he got after our parents died.

Your parents passed away?

Aww, I don't wanna talk about it. So anyway, that twenty, I could buy a case of whiskey at the dock. Cost me $1.25 per bottle, and I'd resell it for $3.

That sounds like a good profit.

Yeah, it was pretty good, yeah. I didn't even have to cross the river. Canadians would buy it. Everyone loves to drink, you know?

They surely do. If you were making good money doing that, why didn't you stay with it?

Hey, that was good if you like to stay small time. Me, I went into the export business. That was what them fancy people in Walkerville called it.

Rumrunning.

Yeah. Moving liquor across the border and then selling it.

That must have been difficult.

First I started out easy, a rowboat with a couple of cases. Let me tell you, it was like a goddamn highway with all of us zipping back and forth. I did it in the winter, too. The law's too slow to grab you then.

Got to be a 24-hour job. I'd hit up different export docks all the time, get paid cash, load up, and set off.

So I started off with a boat. The Detroit River is only a mile across, easy work. I got some other guys working for me, taking old Ford trucks or cars.

That's not what you're famous for, White Lightning.
You got that right. I was the first one to get a plane.
How did you do that?
Well, first of all, I needed a place to store the liquor, plus room for my plane and for takeoff and landing, and that don't always come easy. But I could rent the fields from the farmers, in a way. I gave them a case of beer—that's a lot of money, you know—
Sure is.
So I give them a whole case, save them twenty dollars. If they need a bottle to celebrate a baby, no problem. I'd pass them a bottle of whisky, no charge. Sometimes they need a whole keg for a wedding. I can take care of that.

So they said go ahead, use our fields. I got four fields that way, plus our brother's farm, you know. He let me use that for free.

Yes, I understand you used the five fields for the export business. That was how you met Al Capone?

Yeah, you heard about that. Everyone heard about that. I met him twice.

What was that like?

Everyone wants to know about Al. Okay, well, he's the one who comes to see me. He and one of his guys came up to the dock and asked who could handle that for him.

Didn't he already have people?

Sure he did. He had a lot of boats. I knew some of the guys who were getting it to him. But he wanted a plane every day. I was the only one who could handle that.

We talked in our farmhouse. I showed them the cellar, and I told them, "I'm not fooling around. I know every move you make in Chicago."

He said, "How'd you know Chicago?"

"Hey, you came to me because I got connections. I know people in government. You mess with me, your goose is cooked. I'm White Lightning. Got that?"

"Yeah."

I agreed with him. "Yeah."

Weren't you scared of a well-known gangster like Al Capone?

He was a businessman. I understood that. If I brought him what he wanted, and he paid me, he had nothing to complain about.

I heard you did more than business with Mr. Capone.

I don't know what you mean. He was good to work with. He had his own bombers to work with.

Bombers?

Yeah, old bomber airplanes. Each one of them had a long pit in there, big enough for 25 cases of whiskey!

Twenty-five cases?

Yeah, in one plane. Every morning, at 6 am, a man and the pilot would meet up in one of my fields. Sometimes the temp would drop to ten below. Didn't matter. I was there loading the plane up.

What was your set-up?

Capone ordered what he needed from the export dock and had it delivered to one of my five fields. I'd meet the plane wherever it landed. The pilot would hand me a bank bundle of money. The amount was stamped on the back by the bank. I threw it on the floor of my car.

You didn't count it?

Count it, hell. No time. They gave me five lousy minutes to load the plane. Every morning, I'd be loading 25 cases, which means 300 bottles of whiskey.

So what was the other time you met Capone?

Hardly saw him that time.

I heard that you flew down to Chicago, to Sportsman's Park Racetrack.

I got no memory of that. Anyway, you got enough stuff about the old times. Send me a copy when you're done.

~

I TAPPED THE PAPER. "Strange way to end the interview. Something happened in Chicago when he met Capone the second time."

Tucker nodded. "Agreed. I wonder if that's why @no_bull sent me a picture of Al Capone."

"Maybe." I texted Tori my suspicions about the second meeting. She replied, *Got it.*

"What if that's how he died?" I asked Tucker. "He met Al Capone—"

"Makes a good headline, but we don't know anything about that."

I nodded. "And whatever happened the second time, he survived long enough to give this interview."

"There's more to it, though." Tucker started rereading the article. "That's why they brought me in here. They know, and they want me to find out. So Al Capone is a clue. People calling me White Lightning is a clue. I just have to put it all together."

"The problem is, everyone from Prohibition is dead," I said.

Tucker looked up from the article. "Not whoever messaged me."

"Yeah, if only we could get a hold of @no_bull_1920_. I've got to admit, I have no idea how to research this when everyone else is dead." I tapped my teeth with my index finger until I realized how unsanitary that was. Tucker grinned at me as he noticed.

I rolled my eyes at him. "I bet Josie knows something. You should talk to her."

"I'm on it. I'll concentrate on her at the ball. She'll be my number two woman, after you."

17

EDWIN

As Edwin pulled himself onto the roof, he prayed for rain, snow, or hail to cool down the chimney. Better yet, lightning would strike Mr. Bagnell. Edwin could escape.

The sky stayed cloudy without a hint of rain, and Mr. Bagnell didn't bother to climb to the roof after Edwin.

Edwin shivered despite the morning sun rising into the sky. He swayed slightly in the wind, and for a second he imagined himself flying free. Then Mr. Bagnell bawled, "Mind the pipe. There's an iron pipe projecting into the flue. You got to move around that."

Edwin's toes gripped the roof as he made his way to the chimney. The quicker they did each job, the sooner they could move onto the next.

A foot away, he could feel the heat baking the tiles under his soles and rising through the air toward him.

"Master, it's too hot," he called down.

Mr. Bagnell raised his fist without speaking. He had beaten Edwin so many times that the boy could anticipate the meaty fist clouting his ear, his kidneys, or his stomach.

Edwin's stomach ached with constant hunger, a pain that he'd grown accustomed to, as he stared into the chimney opening. It looked almost too narrow for him to fit. The boys had told him that a chimney was supposed to be a brick and a half wide, but sometimes they were only a brick wide, or 9 inches by 9 inches, at the top.

Edwin pulled off his shirt and breeches and dropped them beside the chimney. That was what his friend Walter had told him to do if it looked too small. And Henry had said it was a good idea to buff it anyway, in case his clothes got caught on snags.

Edwin pulled his climbing cap low over his eyes, to protect him from the soot.

"Get in there, you rummon, before I knock you in!" Mr. Bagnell bawled.

18

HOPE

When we entered the attic bar, where they held the ball, the Star Wars stormtroopers theme blasted from a speaker on either end of the bar. Tucker pretended to play the trumpet, and I laughed.

I needn't have worried about his outfit. He fit right in. It was me, in my jeans and a white shirt, who looked like a Boomer who'd stumbled into the wrong set.

This was only accentuated when they switched to a song I'd never heard before, "The Eggsecutioner," but everyone around me started dancing and mouthing the words.

So I blocked out the noise and concentrated on the costumes and makeup around me. My main problem was that at first, I hardly recognized any characters. I don't have time to watch movies. It's all I can do to keep up with medicine and read children's books for fun.

Still, I recognized the guy in fishnets from The Rocky Horror Picture Show, because our high school once had a showing where my friend drew VIRGIN on my forehead with her eyeliner. Tonight's sweet transvestite pranced around on high heels better than I ever would.

On the other hand, I couldn't figure out why someone was dressed as a green-eyed lion.

"Scar from The Lion King," Tucker murmured to me, his eyes gleaming. He loved this stuff. "I'm pretty sure the other one, the leopard, is Tai Lung from Kung Fu Panda."

"Not half as scary as the woman from Misery!" I whispered back. An overweight woman with a simple bob, a blue patterned blouse, and a brown smock dress freaked me out even without the long, sharp knife.

I blinked at one short woman's button eyes. Literally buttons for eyes, since she wore a black headband that blended into her black hair, and the button eyes dangled from the headband, almost like sunglasses. I recognized her from Coraline because I enjoy Neil Gaiman's books.

That teenager wearing a bra and underwear with cotton balls glued onto them cut in front of Coraline's Other Mother and purred, "Hello, dear," at Tucker.

He kept a respectful distance. "Hi."

"Can I get you something?" She placed one hand on one slim hip. She looked barely pubertal, with a flat ass and breasts smaller than mine.

"No, thanks." Tucker guided me past her, not stopping until we reached the other side of the room.

"I guess she could have been a server," I said doubtfully.

He raised his eyebrows.

"She hardly looked sixteen," I agreed.

Miss Trunchbull swaggered through the crowd and paused at me. "Girl, why bother with cloud when you could have the whole storm right here?" She turned her considerable assets around and twerked at me, two hard beats that made my mouth drop open.

Miss Trunchbull whirled away, and I turned to Tucker, who laughed. "You're easy to tease."

I resolved to keep up a more poker face as I surveyed the rest of the crowd.

At least three Medusas had rigged up snake hair, one more

successful than the others—I kept my distance from the one who seemed to have used coat hangers, which looked great but I kept imagining her puncturing my eyeballs. Bellatrix Lestrange sipped her martini with a wand in her dominant hand, daring the crowd to come closer.

The Wicked Witch of the West was pretty easy to figure out too. The book *Wicked* waits in my To Be Read pile, and I may never make it to the musical, but childhood me got to watch *The Wizard of Oz*.

Some Nightmare Before Christmas characters danced by a little too close to me.

Numerous people dressed up from Game of Thrones. I'd read the books until they depressed me. So I recognized a few Lannisters, including a child dressed as Tyrion. Weird!

I was most impressed by the non-human entries, including Audrey II, the man-eating flower from Little Shop of Horrors. She of the Venus fly trap head and two rows of teeth would reach out with two tentacles to pluck a beer out of someone's hand or ruffle a kid's hair.

That made me check out the minors. One was a blond girl in a red dress with a white collar who stood blank-faced. The dark-haired boy beside her glared at me from under his wide-brimmed hat—not sure what he was, but I gave him a wide berth.

I noted the cotton ball girl was now talking to a man with a wispy salt-and-pepper wig who seemed to have too many teeth. The only one who made me laugh was the baby dressed up as Stewie Griffin from the Family Guy. His dad was dressed as Brian, the dog. Oh, and the Home Alone kid wasn't too scary either.

I smiled. Usually I work up to 36 hours in a row at the hospital, which kills your sense of humour and your ability to do, well, anything fun. Meanwhile, these people had spent hours, days, maybe months of their lives studying and replicating some of their favourite characters, all for the joy of one weekend. They got to be someone or something else, and hang out with other like-minded people, for less than 72 hours.

I got it. In fact, I felt a little at home.

Tucker pulled out his phone to shoot a video of the crowd. Most of them posed. Some pretended not to see him, including the bald guy with a combover whose gaze passed over us, heavy with indifference, as he pushed a cart into the room. Part of his costume? Who knew.

"That's the man from Hush," said Tucker, nodding at the guy in the white face mask. "His crossbow's wrong, though. The one in the movie wasn't all metal."

I'd never heard of Hush, but the face mask was creepy, with holes for the eyes, a straight nose, and a slight, closed smile for the mouth. I glanced at the steel crossbow. "I guess he did the best he could. Probably not the easiest thing to get a crossbow."

"Especially a fake one for a con," Tucker agreed.

The music changed. I recognized "I'll Be Back" from Hamilton, and I belted the chorus along with everyone else. Tucker sang with his eyes closed.

As the song wound down, I edged toward the entrance. The combover guy growled as I approached his cart, but I didn't care. I could have dressed up like Sherlock Holmes, or maybe Moriarty. That might make the "detective doctor" moniker less like a curse and more funny, almost like an ugly donkey piñata we could marvel over before we destroyed it together.

Then the deep chords of Beethoven's Fifth rubbed the air, and I stopped short.

A villain soared ahead of me, carried by four different guys on what looked like a tray with four posts on the end. I think it's called a litter.

The guys wore masks from Alien, the movie with Sigourney Weaver where aliens were basically teeth and a bullet-like forehead. But those guys faded from my consciousness, for their leader stepped down from her tray, aided by two more men.

You know those dance moves where you spread out your arms in a T and the guys take your arms and lower you down gracefully? Like that, which I'd never seen before in real life. She flowed down to the ground.

Chapter 18

And it was a she, I knew that instinctively, even though her back faced me, and I could hardly make out her hips or backside because of the knife-like projections spiking toward me along her entire spine.

Tucker and I jostled our way back into the room to see her front.

The music flipped to something instrumental and sad, which might have detracted from her show, because there were no words and no beat, only strings and what might have been an oboe calling out the melody, but somehow, that made it even more special.

I maneuvered my way to the front of the growing throng and gaped at her massive, engraved, insect-like forehead piece that made her a foot taller than me.

She was an alien too, but I knew she was the queen who ruled them all.

19

EDWIN

Edwin clambered on top of the chimney, finding his balance first. Lucky he was always good at balancing, as long as he could remember. His mum used to call him her little monkey.

"Go on!"

Edwin could hear the brewhouse men's voices through the chimney, but mostly he could smell the smoke and already feel the soot lighting on his skin.

He reached down to grasp the lip of the chimney before dangling his feet into the flue, and then he gasped.

It was the hottest he'd ever felt, like the flames of Hell.

Still, he climbed down, brushing with his left hand as he descended, bracing himself with his right arm, both legs, and his back. Layers of soot and creosote fell on him and past him.

He squeezed his eyes shut, but not fast enough. His eyes streamed with tears from more dirt and soot.

He braced his knees against the sides of the chimney as he coughed, trying not to suck any more grit up his lungs, even though it was still hot enough to burn his nose hairs.

The lower he went, the hotter the bricks became. Then something seared his right foot.

20

HOPE

She stood on two delicate feet covered in shoes that reminded me of horns, with tiny, matching pink talons on her hands and feet. Then she opened her jaws.

Mucous stretched between her teeth. We all gasped.

Her entire body had become her costume, from her helmet-like head to the ironwork covering her torso and the boots that traversed her thighs. She even had a tail extending behind her, a segmented thing that curled toward her knees.

Hot breath exhaled toward me, a final detail that almost made me scream.

Some people did.

The bra/panties/cotton ball girl prostrated herself on the ground beside me. "Rest in peace, Queen!" she yelled, which didn't make sense to me, but the music was cranked, we were packed together, and the girl could be high or drunk or both.

The queen seemed to shimmer in her costume, and after a few beats, I realized she was dancing. She oozed sensuality as she lifted her arms in the air and swayed her hips.

I could stare at her all day.

I have never hooked up with a woman, let alone someone I've never seen, but at that moment, I would. We all would. I glanced at Tucker and recognized the hunger on his face.

I didn't resent it. Might as well resent gravity.

The music died with one final trembling note.

The queen held her position, her hips cocked to her right and her arms swept skyward.

The combover guy abandoned his cart and stumbled toward her, brandishing a bouquet of flowers.

Weird. Had he hidden the flowers on his cart, under the drape?

The queen didn't react. Her hands probably weren't functional.

One of her bodyguard men stepped forward and took the bouquet.

Or he tried. Combover Guy shook his head, insistent, before he wrestled the bouquet away from the bodyguard.

Two more bodyguards stepped forward, forming a wall in front of their queen.

"You can't give her the flowers, buddy!" called Miss Trunchbull behind me.

Combover Guy took two steps forward, switching the bouquet to his left hand so he could jab the bodyguard in the chest with his index finger.

"Ooh," said everyone.

"Hey!" I called. We were all tense, drunk, disturbed by the skeleton in the chimney, trapped in our costumes, and trying to impress the queen. We were one wrong move away from a full-on brawl.

The murmurs grew louder.

Tucker took up the call. "Relax!"

Instead, the crowd pressed closer. Whether they wanted to beat up combover guy, climb on the queen, or both, tension seethed throughout the room.

The alien queen held up one imperious hand.

We stilled, except the guards, whom she gestured aside. Silence reigned.

Chapter 20

The queen stretched her hand toward the flowers. Combover Guy clutched them in his trembling hand before the queen's maw opened, and then her jaws closed over the bouquet.

We stood in stunned silence as the entire bouquet disappeared in her mouth.

21

"Holy—"

"Amazing! Amazing!"

"Did you get that?"

"How did she do it?"

The guy in the white mask applauded, and the rest of us joined in, dazzled, as the litter slowly retreated.

For the first time, I thought I might spend my next vacation at a con. Done well, it was like magic.

The DJ cranked up the music—an amped up version of "All That Jazz," which somehow seemed fitting—and Jennifer winked at us as she rushed around serving drinks.

Slowly, people shook off their queen haze and started dancing again. I joined them, but I felt off. I wanted to follow the queen.

I couldn't see the cotton ball girl. Maybe she'd set off without me noticing. I twisted around to check.

"Hey!"

Griffin whipped around to face Combover Guy, who had bumped him with his trolley.

Weird. Did Combover Guy work here? But then I remembered

Jennifer asking if she could help him with his cart. He was a guest. Maybe the cart was part of his rogue outfit.

Combover Guy held up an apologetic hand and backed up.

"Hey," Tucker called, but Combover Guy retreated with his cart while muttering to himself

Combover Guy didn't fit in with the other Rogue Conners. If there were 120 people here, no one except him looked over 30, and he looked twice that.

Why did this man crash the party and offer flowers to the alien queen?

On the other hand, I'd been tempted to offer her flowers, or more.

"Wait, I want to talk to you!" Tucker called after Combover Guy, who maneuvered his cart through the crowd.

"Leave it, Tucker," I said, still thinking.

Deep down, we're all animals. Sometimes we want a leader, someone to take us by the hand and make it all okay.

Sometimes we want someone to fuck.

The alien queen was all the more hypnotizing because she was both, melded into one.

Tucker raced after Combover Guy, who was pretty easy to catch because of the cart. "Hey, how's it going?" Tucker yelled above the music. "I like your costume. Who did you dress up as?"

Combover Guy nosed through the door, mumbling something that sounded like "Lou Goneys."

"Ah, Leopoldo Lugones?" Tucker rattled off some Spanish at Combover Guy's back.

"Who was Leopoldo Lugones?" I asked, trying to imitate Tucker's flow and intonation.

The hallway was noticeably quieter and cooler, and we watched Combover Guy check his phone as he waited for the elevator with his precious cart.

Tucker smiled and snapped a picture of Combover Guy before he turned back to me. "Lugones is considered one of the greatest Spanish-language writers and poets. He ushered in the era of modernism. His birthday is *Día del escritor*, the Day of the Writer, in Argentina."

Yikes. I'd never heard of this poet. "How's he a rogue?"

"I don't know," Tucker admitted. "One of the staff doctors used to quote his poetry all the time, though."

"Like what?"

"I remember there was one called *'Historia De Mi Muerte.'* 'The Story of My Death.'"

"Well, that's cheerful." I gave Tucker the side eye as the elevator binged, an elderly lady disembarked, and Combover Guy carefully backed into the elevator with his cart. "So you think 'Lugones' is the one sending you messages?"

Tucker's eyes flashed before he suppressed his reaction. "Why'd you say that?"

"No way you liked his costume. Why, are you going to buzz off 90 percent of your hair and comb two strands over your bald pate? Unlikely."

"I could try a different look. Lugones wouldn't always have been bald."

I rolled my eyes. "Look, I don't care if you want to interview every Rogue and his cat. But I think you're better off questioning Josie Tucker. Is she really related to you?"

"I'm working on all angles," Tucker said. "I set up a rapport with 'Lugones.' I can always reach out to him later, now that he trusts me."

"Yeah, any second now, he'll be whipping back the drapes on his cart to show you his franks and beans."

Tucker waggled his eyebrows at me. I tell you, he's always good to go.

"Seriously," I said, "that guy is weird. The way he acts so protective of his cart—even when he was staring at the queen, he kept one hand on his cart."

"I'll give him some therapy while I interview him," said Tucker. "For now, let's party."

22

EDWIN

Edwin screamed like he'd never screamed before, and then he was sliding in the chimney, almost dropping the brush, scraping his back and his buttocks and his hands and his knees, trying to stay up, trying to stay away, but now his left leg hit that thing too, and he screamed some more.

The pipe. The iron pipe.
Still deadly hot from the fire.
Like the devil's hand taking off his leg.

Edwin remembered George's legs, the smell of the pus bubbling on them, and whipped both his own legs up as high as he could take them.

Faintly, Edwin heard voices from the brewhouse, and Mr. Bagnell calling, "Come up, boy. Come back!"

More soot and grit rained down on Edwin before something thumped on his head and right shoulder, startling him enough to make him slide down a few more inches.

Mr. Bagnell had thrown him a rope, but now Edwin was wedged with his knees near his chin. He could hardly breathe, let alone grasp the rope and maneuver out of the chimney.

With great effort, Edwin gathered his words together. "I cannot come up, master, I must die here."

He felt dizzy. Nothing mattered so much anymore. The heat now felt inevitable, almost comforting, instead of the white hot flashes of agony.

In the distance, his mother sang for her little monkey.

Edwin closed her eyes so he could hear her better.

23

HOPE

"I'd love to party!" hollered an elderly voice.

Uh oh. I hadn't looked closely enough at who'd come out of the elevator—clearly they'd added that since 1928—and boom. Josie Tucker hastened toward us with only a slight limp in her right leg.

"Did I miss anything?" she asked, her eyes on Tucker.

"The alien queen," I said.

She blinked in confusion, but Tucker covered beautifully. "The party starts with you. Would you care to dance?" He offered her his left arm.

"I'd love to!" She hurried toward the bar, nearly dragging him down with her first stumble.

Tucker shot me an apologetic look, but I waved them to the dance floor. She was supposed to be an elderly relation, if only in her own mind—with a matching ID. Forgery seemed a bit much for a senior citizen's costume.

After P. Diddy's "Bad Boys for Life" crashed to a close, Tucker returned without Josie.

"Lose your girlfriend?" Griffin joked.

Tucker shook his head and pointed at me. "She's right here."

I tucked my arm around him, comforted for no clear reason. "Did you have fun?"

"Yeah, actually. I love seeing old people, especially when they've got all their neurons and can take a spin around the dance floor."

"And if they can educate you about your family tree?" I asked.

Tucker shrugged. "She thinks we're related. We've got the same last name and the same hair. Everyone in our family goes white before they're 30."

"I never knew that before," said Tori.

"Yeah, I don't make a big deal out of it. Most people think I'm blond."

"Why didn't you tell me?" I said. I hadn't clued in because his sisters are younger and still regular blonde, and his father shaved his head after going bald, a potential future that haunts Tucker. I knew my guy had white hair, but I thought he was either naturally super Aryan or into bleach. My bad.

I changed tacks. The white hair could be a genetic link, or a genetic giveaway. "What about her conviction that she, and therefore Tucker, are related to master bootlegger White Lightning? It was dumb of WL to call attention to his most visible trait, though. He could've called himself Drunken Wings or Fly Me to the Gin or something."

Tori raised her eyebrows at me.

"That was a bad one," I admitted. "But you get my point."

"It might not have been avoidable," said Griffin, to my surprise. "People call me Black Boy or Kaffir or whatever they want."

My mouth fell open. I'd read a South African autobiography, so I knew the latter was the equivalent of the N word.

"If they're going to call you that, you might as well run with it," Griffin told him. "Beats them calling you by your real name."

"Probably," said Tucker.

I shook my head. "Anyway, did she say anything while you were dancing?"

"She wouldn't admit that she'd messaged me. Claimed she didn't know Instagram."

Chapter 23

I snorted. Kind of hard not to hear about IG, even in passing. "And she still says you're related?"

"Oh, I know we are," Josie's voice crackled behind me. Yikes. I nearly jumped as Josie bore down on us as fast as she could, saying, "I was only playing with him." She paused. "That's what you kids say, isn't it? Playing with you?"

I ignored that. "How do you know that you're related?"

"Genealogy is one of my passions. I've traced my lineage all the way back to 1832, in Derby."

"In England?"

"Of course." She looked a bit snooty. "The birthplace of the industrial revolution, by the banks of the River Derwent."

Ugh. I hated to imagine the pollution clogging that river, but I needed to quiz her. "What did you find in 1832?"

"Our ancestor became a chimney sweep, or a climbing boy, as they were known, in 1838. He was born in 1832."

I licked my lips. No way. It *couldn't* be, of all the child labourers during the Industrial Revolution. But it would explain so much. I shot Tori a look. She shook her head, so I was the one to casually inquire, "Was his name Edwin?"

Josie shook her head.

I shoved my disappointment away. "Do you know his name, then?"

She grinned. "Of course I do."

And she was going to make me beg for it. "What is it?"

"You might have heard of him. He became quite famous. He started out as an orphan before he was apprenticed as a chimney sweep. You have no idea the amount of work they had to do—"

"I have some," I said quietly.

"No, you do not. They were starved. They risked getting burned, getting stuck and suffocating in the chimneys. If they survived, they got cancer."

I nodded, thinking of those poor little mites. "I'm sorry."

Josie tilted her head back so she could stare down her nose at me. "Nothing to be sorry about. It's not as if you had anything to do with it."

"Quite." I sounded more British already. "Do you have any documentation about your ancestor?"

She offered the nose-look again. "I'll give it to John next time. I don't trust e-mail for that sort of sensitive information."

"Thank you," said Tucker, instead of telling her that he preferred being called by his last name, the way he told everyone else.

"Why is it sensitive?" Tori asked quietly.

"Oh, some of it is quite fascinating. We still have his card, 'Chimney Sweeper to Her Royal Highness the Princess Louise Caroline Alberta' that said he could 'rectify and cure smoakey chimneys.'" She smiled. "He spelled it s-m-o-a-k-e-y. He must have been extremely good at it because he guaranteed his work: 'no cure no pay.'"

I frowned. "You said he was in Derby. How did he manage to sweep the princess's chimney?" While Josie drew her chin back, I went on, "Did she visit from London, or did he go to London to tend to her chimney there?"

She cleared her throat. "My goodness, you ask so very many questions."

In other words, he probably never swept any princess's chimney.

She read the disbelief on my face, drew herself up to her full five-foot height (still over two inches shorter than me!) and proclaimed, "He was considered a master sweep. Only 20 of his compatriots reached that level in London, let alone in the East Midlands."

"Uh huh."

"Oh, I can see you won't believe anything. Here you go."

She fumbled in her wallet and finally withdrew a card enclosed in a plastic case. I couldn't be sure through the plastic, but the paper did look yellowed and worn, with lettering difficult to read.

I could, however, make out her relative's name:

J O H N T U C K E R

24

CLOUD

She didn't expect it to hurt.
"It's your first time?" he asked as he unlocked the wooden door with the blue star on it, waving her into the suite. "That's what she told me. You are ... fresh."

Ew. She forced herself to smile. "If you say so."

Was the air conditioning on? This room was so cold. She tried not to shiver.

"Aren't you a pretty girl," he whispered, and then he started talking in something else, maybe French, while he closed the door behind her.

The honeymoon suite smelled a bit like pine trees. She stepped on the wooden floor and goosebumps sprang up on her arms.

It's going to be okay, *she told herself.* J said she'd check on me in an hour.

He hurried past her and the bathroom to the left. She felt the wood walls pressing in on her. Sure, he'd make a run for the back right wall, with the king bed that was covered in a quilt with blue and white stars. She forced a smile on her face.

Wait. The guy twisted sideways. Maybe he was going for the bedside table to the right of the bed. Its yellow and green stained glass lamp made a circle of light in the room.

No. He stopped even sooner, at some sort of cart. He peeked under the black sheet covering its contents, then readjusted the sheet, humming to himself.

All she could see was the bottom of the cart's steel frame and its wheels sticking out from under the sheet, but it sure seemed to make him happy.

She knew that already. The guy had brought a fucking cart to the dance floor. Probably not the smartest tool in the box. But that was okay. J said those were easier. You can make 'em do what you want.

He turned away from the cart and studied her. She still hadn't moved from the door, but he said, "You are so beautiful."

Was she supposed to tell him that he was cute, too? The lie seized up in her throat.

"Nice room," she said finally. The honeymoon suite was huge. It felt bigger than the two-bedroom apartment she shared with four other people. She could sleep all day in that bed, waking up only for room service or to watch movies on the flat screen TV on the opposite wall.

J had told her there was a water spa (whatever that was) next door that was open to everyone until midnight, but the honeymoon suite had a lockable sliding door, so she could sneak in there after hours. "And you can see the lake from your window!"

Massive room. "Water spa" access. Lakeside view. She couldn't complain about any of that, or about the cold, hard cash that she'd pinned in her bra.

All she had to do was to put up with this guy for an hour. His hair, the remaining strings on his head, made her want to puke, so she thought of the water spa instead.

"Yes. It will make a beautiful backdrop." He held up his phone and said, "I need to immortalize you." Then he cooed more foreign stuff that made her skin crawl.

She rubbed her arms, trying to warm herself up, trying to make herself walk over to him. Was it okay if he filmed her? Should she charge more? But she didn't do the money stuff. J took care of that.

He switched back to English. "I will treasure you forever, my little one. I will protect you. Now take off your clothes and put on new ones."

He walked around the bed so he was standing between it and the enormous windows overseeing the lake. Then he pointed at the lingerie laid out on the bed. It looked like a white corset attached to a white thong.

Ugh. She'd rather keep her bra with the cash. But she forced her legs to walk toward him and his costume. She touched the bed, and the mattress moved under her hand. She screamed before she could stop herself.

He laughed. "It is a waterbed. A special treat for you."

She picked up the corset and underwear while he said, "You are so beautiful, so precious. I will enjoy making you mine."

She made a sound that passed as a laugh, but she couldn't help glancing at the cart to her right and behind. What was he hiding?

"You want to see?" His voice hummed with pleasure as he knelt on the bed and reached forward to touch her hair.

She forced herself not to shudder as he brushed her bangs out of her eyes and ended by stroking her ear.

"Your skin is so soft, my curious one. Yes, you are perfect. You are like a little white mouse, and I am ready to give you your piece of cheese."

She bit back a laugh. What the hell was he talking about? But maybe it was okay to giggle. J said, "Laugh, smile, make 'em feel good."

He chuckled under his breath.

"Yes, like that. Perfect." He snapped five pictures with his phone before zooming in on her face. "I must have a video. You are too much. I will keep a record of you and guard it with my life."

She bared her teeth. This was worse than school pics in front of a green screen. Her heart bucked in her chest.

I gotta get out of here.

No. J had said this guy checked out.

She had to give him an hour. No big deal. Pics were better than touching him, right?

She couldn't help how her breath caught in her throat. The room air still felt like ice. She crossed her arms over her stupid nipples.

"Ah, ah." The guy climbed to his feet, pulled her arms open again, and filmed her nipples and her crotch. "Cold, are you?"

She nodded, trying not to shiver.

"Don't worry, my little darling. I brought an electric blanket. It's already plugged in." He pointed at a neatly folded beige blanket on the bedside table, in front of the lamp. The blanket's black and grey controller stuck out between two layers. The controller light glowed red, showing that it was on.

"I'll even turn it up for you. You can have it ... after." His voice dipped, and she tried not to imagine what he meant by that.

Her eyes drifted toward the cart to the right and behind her. Why'd he push it around the dance floor? Who did that?

He took more pictures as he spoke. "They say curiosity killed the cat, but I think you're a smart kitten. You want to know the surprise. Why wouldn't you? Well, because you've been so good, I might give you a taste."

He started toward the cart, passing by her with less than a foot to spare. She was grateful that he didn't touch her again. He smelled strange, metallic and like old rubber.

Before he reached the cart, he stared at his screen and cursed quietly under his breath. "My phone is almost out of battery. I used it more than I expected earlier. Foolish of me. Fortunately, I brought a charger." He grinned at her like he expected her to join in.

She swallowed. "I'm only here for an hour."

"Darling, I can keep you here as long as I want. As long as I pay you. That's what she said. Didn't you hear her?"

She licked her lips. "She said to stay for an hour."

He sighed. "You've barely gotten here, little mouseling. Stay. Be with me. I assure you the experience will be ... unforgettable." He started talking foreign again, and she nodded and smiled and clutched the clothes while secretly hoping she wasn't leaving sweat marks on the fabric of the shitty outfit he wanted her to wear.

"We'll have to stay close so I can charge my phone," he said. "There's a whirlpool bath next door. Wouldn't you like to dip your pretty toes? I'd like to film you doing that." His breathing was so loud that it would embarrass her to sound like that, but he didn't seem to care.

What was she doing here? She gulped, and he filmed that too. She was starting to hate the camera he kept locked on her.

"Give me a moment, sweetness." He passed his precious cart and reached for a grey duffel bag that he must've placed earlier on the luggage

Chapter 24

holder closer to the door. He took his time unzipping the bag. "I know I have that charger somewhere." He sighed. "Here's the cord. I don't know how it got frayed."

As he clucked over his damaged USB cable, she gazed over his shoulder into the depths of his duffel bag and went very still. She'd spotted a knife.

25

HOPE

Josie waved at us and limped to the bathroom while I processed the name of Tucker's supposed ancestor. Had he really been a master sweep, or was this a fake calling card?

I whipped around when Tori gasped.

"What is it?" I asked, but she silently buried her head in Griffin's chest. I darted to her side to try to catch her eye.

"Are you okay?" asked Tucker.

Tori's dark head seemed to nod into Griffin's shirt. "I just remembered something."

"What?" I mouthed at her once her eyes resurfaced.

Tori shook her head. Griffin murmured to her, and she nodded and turned to face us with a fake smile, Griffin's arms still locked around her. "I'll explain that later. First, I know what happened at the second meeting between Al Capone and White Lightning."

I went along with it. "Already?"

She nodded and held her phone up as reference. "A pilot came to get White Lightning and said, 'Capone wants you to come to Chicago.' They flew to Chicago's Sportsman's Park Racetrack. White Lightning joined Capone's car, heralded by three motorcycles in front and

Chapter 25

flanked by three motorcycles in back. 'I want to show you a good time tonight,' Capone said."

My shoulders tensed. What would a top gangster consider a good time?

"White Lightning spoke for weeks about the 'beautiful show' of 50 girls, 'young girls, sixteen, seventeen.'"

I cringed, and Tori nodded in agreement.

"Might have been legal back then," Tucker said.

"It's still legal, if all they do is dance," I said, but I had a bad feeling about this.

"He said afterward that it was the best night of his life," Griffin said.

I rolled my eyes at Tori, but she'd bent over her phone to double check. "He said he drank so much that he couldn't remember who and where he was."

So White Lightning had blacked out, but he could have done a lot of damage before he went unconscious.

"He woke up in the morning when a man with a machine gun tapped him on the shoulder. 'Come on. Put your pants on. You got to get back. Pick up that load.' White Lightning was so hung over, he could hardly get his pants on."

Yuck.

"He needed a drink. The man with a machine gun gave him a shot of whisky. 'Here's your drink. After your pants.' Then the man drove White Lightning to the airport, and White flew back to Belle River."

A drunk White Lightning had definitely taken his pants off during or after a night out with fifty young girls. It could have been as innocent as needing to take a leak. Or as vile as him violating multiple underage girls.

Whatever he'd done, was it enough to make someone want to kill him?

"I'll send you the reference. It's from a book called *The Rumrunners*, by Charles Henry Gervais," said Tori. "The author interviewed a number of rumrunners before they died."

"He interviewed White Lightning?"

"He sure did. There's a whole section on him."

Tori had already bought the book, so I borrowed her phone to read a few pages. While a song apparently named "DoucheBag" played at the ball, I came across something else. "Here's a better picture of him."

Tucker and I bent our heads over the greyscale photo of a man wearing a suit, white shirt, a tie, and a tidy straw hat with a ribbon around its base. The hair under the hat looked pure white, like Draco Malfoy white. And something about his eyes and crooked smile reminded me of my guy.

Tucker's fingers trembled. "He looks a bit like my dad."

"It's all speculation for now," I said, trying to keep my guy calm.

He turned to Tori. "Can I talk to Charles Henry Gervais?"

She looked startled. "You could try."

"I'm going to look him up," said Tucker, punching the buttons on his phone a little harder than necessary.

"Hang on," said Griffin, studying his own phone. "There's a whole thing here about White Lightning and the Purple Gang in Detroit."

"That makes sense, since it's right across the river," said Tucker, without looking up. "That's a hell of a lot closer than Chicago. What does it say about the Purple Gang?"

"He said, 'They're tough, but they don't bother me.'" Griffin used his finger to scroll down. He was a slower reader than Tori. After a minute, Griffin said, "He went over to their bar. He'd knock on the door and the bouncer would say, 'Who do you want to see?' But as soon as they got a look at him, they'd say, 'Hello, White Lightning! Let him in.' And they'd bring him champagne or whatever he wanted."

"Interesting," said Tori.

I frowned. How did that tie into White Lightning's death or disappearance? And then I had it. "Would the Purple Gang have gotten pissed off that he was selling to Al Capone too? Weren't they rivals?"

"How'd you know that, Hope? You blow my mind." Tucker pressed a hearty kiss on my neck.

I grinned and kissed him back. "Hey, I can figure out gang rivalry."

Chapter 25

Griffin made a face. "Says here White Lightning sold to Capone, the Purple Gang, plus some connection in Philly."

"So there was a *third* group he sold to?" My heart sank. How could we figure out who was at the bottom of the chimney, let alone whoever put him or her there, without forensic anthropology and DNA testing? Especially after 100 years?

"Wouldn't surprise me if he kept selling to smaller customers on the side too. Guys like this never stop," said Griffin.

Made sense. I wondered how Griffin knew that, but I didn't know him well enough to pry.

Tori's cool voice broke in. "They say it's usually someone close to you who kills you. Your partner is the first suspect. Women are often victims of intimate partner violence."

"That's true," I said sadly. "So we should investigate Gertrud, in case she was involved, and any other partners of White Lightning. He could have done something in Chicago with those girls. Then he could have killed Gertrud if she confronted him about it."

"Or someone killed him," said Griffin.

Tori nodded. "As a rumrunner, I imagine he would have been at higher risk than a tavern owner, even a female tavern owner."

"We should consider that the bones could be either of them, or neither of them," I conceded. "But if it was White Lightning because he wronged Al Capone, they wouldn't fly back here and shove him up a chimney. It's not like they had frequent flyer miles back then. They left the flying up to him."

Griffin shrugged. "Capone ran a huge organization. If 75 percent of liquor came through Windsor to Detroit, I bet he'd have fingers on this side of the border."

Tori nodded, touching his sleeve. "Even if Gertrud wanted White Lightning dead, she didn't have to kill him herself. She could have had her employee do it."

"She could have," I admitted, "but that's someone who'd turn on her easily, blackmailing her. She wasn't like the mob with a hundred hit men to keep you in line."

"She did disappear in 1946," Tori said.

"True." Had I figured it out by thinking aloud? Gertrud's accomplice killed White Lightning at her behest, but the accomplice could have blackmailed Gertrud, so she left town ... almost two decades later.

"Blood is thicker than water," said Griffin.

I didn't get the connection, but Tori nodded. "What if it wasn't an employee who killed White Lighting, but someone who had a personal stake? What if WL hurt one of those young girls in Chicago, and a brother or a father followed him up to Windsor and made sure he'd never do that again?"

Tucker snapped his fingers. "That was how Al Capone got his nickname, Scarface! He was rude to a girl and her brother cut him with his knife. So maybe Capone's pic was a hint that it was Gertrud's brother!"

I'd heard the nickname, but hadn't noticed a big scar on Capone. "Which cheek was it?"

"The left." Tucker brought up another picture and handed me his phone.

Now that I searched for it, the scar was obvious, stretching down like an extra-thin sideburn. "Right. I guess the clue to you could be that subtle. Still, why would you put a body in a chimney? It would make more sense to move the body elsewhere. You know how they joke about concrete shoes? I don't know if that's an actual thing, but we're on the Detroit River. That would be the most obvious place to dump a body. Why did they pick a chimney?"

Tucker pursed his lips. "I think you're right about rivers in general, but not about Hooch Highway. The river is only a mile or two wide here. They used to row out in boats all summer, and when the water froze, they'd drive any old car across it. They'd even skate."

I shook my head, imagining trying to police the shore as possibly hundreds of people set out on foot, boat, or plane every day, all carrying liquor.

"Like this." Tucker pulled up a photo of an unfortunate car. Its passenger wheels and its trailer's wheels had completely fallen through the ice, while a half-dozen men stood by helplessly. "This is from Lake St. Clair, which is the Ontario side of the lake between us and the U.S. Obviously they shouldn't have driven over the ice during breakup, but they did it anyway. You wouldn't want a body to bob up in the middle of that."

"That would be bad," I agreed.

Tori shook her head. "There's another reason that White Lightning might have disappeared." She texted us a different article. "One of White Lightning's planes crashed on the American side."

"What?" I quickly scanned the article. "They said he wasn't the pilot. He was the owner."

"Yes, but it was dangerous work. That was his second plane to crash in one month."

"Jamais deux sans trois," muttered Tucker. Never two without three.

I sighed. White Lightning and Gertrud could have died in so many ways, very few of which resulted in one of them buried in a chimney.

I rubbed my eyes and sighed as the "Asshole" song played in the background. "I need science. Does anyone have a forensic anthropologist on speed dial? They could at least tell us if the pelvis looks male or female."

"Working on it," said Tucker. "They told me it's usually a two month delay for a non-urgent case."

Tori smiled a little. "I guess we're lucky it's not an urgent case."

Yet, I thought to myself.

"I need some air," said Griffin, and we all headed downstairs.

26

CLOUD

She recognized the knife handle. Her stepdad used to have one like it. That was when she realized that she might not get out of the honeymoon suite alive.

She'd heard stuff before. A football player saying that the only good bitch was a dead bitch. An uncle joking about "hoors" dying in an alleyway before her mother shushed him.

Now that could be her. Dying in the fanciest hotel room she'd ever seen. Next door to the water spa.

And she couldn't help thinking, if he kept a knife in his luggage and didn't bother to hide it, what the hell was he covering up on that cart?

She stood between him and the bed, so she switched the corset and thong to her left hand and pointed at the phone charger. "Do you want me to plug that for you? I don't mind."

He smiled at her sweetly. "Yes, honey, I'd love you to bend over and plug that for me."

Before she could scream, he shoved her on the bed. The mattress sloshed under her, her head bobbing on a wave.

She'd never been on a waterbed before, and she wanted to puke now more than ever, but she fought back the urge. If she threw up, he might make her lick it up before he kept going.

Chapter 26

He tsked. "They told me this was a new waterbed. New mattresses are supposed to have anti-wave action."

He was going to knife her, but he was pissed that he didn't get the right waterbed? Jesus.

She struggled for breath, opening her mouth to get more oxygen as he forced her nose and mouth into the quilt.

Was this how she'd die? Smothered into the bed?

The more she moved, the harder he pushed, almost like it turned him on.

She stopped fighting him and thought, What does he want?

She reached behind her with her right hand, not to attack him, but to stroke him. Her fingers grazed the air, petting and fluttering, and he seemed to understand that she wasn't trying to claw him.

He relaxed, inching his hips closer to her.

She found his dick—still soft, she could tell through his pants—but his breathing shifted.

"Oh, you're an eager girl. I like that. I'm not ready for it yet. It will be on the menu." He moved out of reach and she heard a familiar click of plastic on plastic, and then a small thunk.

He'd plugged in his phone charger.

She took a quick step back from the bed and spun around to face him. She'd dropped his stupid outfit when he was smothering her. He didn't seem to notice.

She was shaking.

He wants me for more than an hour.

He has a knife.

God knows what he's got in that cart.

He stretched the charger cord as far as possible so he could pan his phone up and down on her, recording her with his mouth open a little as he zoomed in on key areas.

"Gorgeous. Perfect. Pretty as a picture." He tugged on the cord, trying to get closer as he grumbled, "I should have brought an extension cord. I usually do."

She could run. But he might run faster. He had a knife, and he hadn't used up ten minutes, let alone an hour.

Guys were so easy, *I said.* Tits, ass, stick it in a hole, and done.

I don't want him in my tits, ass, or holes. But she'd made a deal with the devil. No one was going to save her. She'd have to work something out.

What? What could she do?

Something besides letting him smother her.

She exhaled and patted the bed. "Why don't you sit here?"

He raised his eyebrows. He had grey eyes, but mostly she stared at his scraggly eyebrows, the little hairs springing in different directions. If she got out of this alive, she'd ID him through his eyebrows.

She smiled. "Film me, and I'll dance for you."

27

HOPE

The side door exit wouldn't budge.

"Want me to try?" Griffin said, already reaching for it, but I gave it another shove and heard a deep voice say, "Hold on to your panties, honey," before Miss Trunchbull opened the door from the outside.

"Oh, I'm sorry, Miss Trunchbull." I must have run into her with the door as she tucked into the doorway to avoid the rain. I gazed up at her as we filed past her; she was taller than all of us except Griffin. "I didn't realize you were there."

She gave a low laugh and tapped the ash off of her cigarette. "I forgive you, sweetheart. I don't bruise easy. Keep calling me Miss Trunchbull. Missus or Ms. are okay too."

"Got it. She/her pronouns." Tucker smiled at her.

"Oh, I like *you*." She eyed him up and down and took a deep drag off her cigarette, its tip dangerously close to the ends of her windblown wig.

"I like you too," said Tucker easily. "Strange night, isn't it?"

"Rogue Con gone rogue," she agreed, blowing the smoke toward us. Tori took a step closer toward the rain to get away from it.

"Those bones in the chimney are wild, though, right?" I asked.

"We're trying to figure them out. You have any ideas?" Tucker tried.

Miss Trunchbull laughed so hard that she started to cough a dry, rattly smoker's cough. We waited uncomfortably until she waved at us and rasped, "I'm okay. Sheesh, kids these days."

"You seem to be ... experienced." Awkward segue that made her laugh again, so I tried to flip us back on track. "Did you receive any special invitation to come here tonight?"

She shrugged. "I signed up for Rogue Con five months ago."

"A more individualized, customized invitation," said Tucker.

Miss Trunchbull waved her cigarette at him. Since she was half a head taller than him, the cig ended up in his face, but he didn't flinch as she said, "Don't be silly. You think the Alien Queen will issue a personal invitation?"

"You know the Alien Queen?" That interested me too.

She laughed and sucked on her cigarette. "Everyone knows the Alien Queen, babyface. We hope and pray she shows up, but no one can guarantee it."

Tucker and I exchanged glances. "She tours cons?" I asked.

"No. She appears very selectively."

"How many times has she appeared?"

She blew a large, almost perfectly circular smoke ring. My open admiration of it softened her a little. "That's my third time seeing her in seven years."

"Wow. So you don't know who she is?"

She shook her head. "No one does."

Well, that was to be expected. Griffin opened the door again and waved Tori back in, but before Tori stepped across the threshold, Miss Trunchbull spoke around her cigarette.

"I do have a message for White Lightning, though."

Tucker whipped around to face her, immediately intent. I laid my hand on his arm to warn him to play it cool.

Miss Trunchbull shrugged. "I'm quite well-known myself. I get all sorts of messages. Not individual invitations to Rogue Con, mind you." She raised one finely-arched eyebrow at Tucker, who blushed.

Chapter 27

She smiled in satisfaction. "I am rather well-connected, however. They know that if they want to pass the word on, they should talk to me."

She breathed, bringing her large bosom to our attention. I ignored it and asked, "What did they say?"

"'He fell to the ground like an olive tree, young, beautiful, strong, covered with white blossoms, suddenly shattered by a bolt of lightning in a storm.'"

I blinked at her. It sounded like a riddle, and given the circumstances, one that we might have to unravel.

"'He fell to the ground like an olive tree,'" Tucker slowly repeated.

"'... young, beautiful, strong ... shattered by a bolt of lightning,'" I said, trying to remember it so I could look up the source. "And this message was directed at Tucker?"

She shook her head. "I found it in my spam email. Subject: tell white lightning."

I raised my natural eyebrows. "Well, that sounds like it could have been meant for anyone, especially in your spam folder."

"I have a very aggressive spam filter, but the message was directed to one of my ... private emails. They wanted me to get the message."

"Did you reply?" I asked.

"I certainly did. I asked how I was supposed to talk to lightning. No one answered, but I figured it out tonight." She tapped her temple with one bedazzled orange acrylic nail.

"Thank you, Miss Trunchbull," I said, towing Tucker back toward the dance floor with an uneasy final glance at the sky.

White is the colour of death in Chinese culture. So I wasn't crazy about the white blossoms. But my main concern was the threat against my beautiful, young, strong, healthy young man, lured here.

To be shattered.

By a bolt of lightning.

28

CLOUD

She tried pitching her voice low and sultry, like J, as she swayed her hips. "You got some music?"

His lips parted as he stared between her legs.

Ugh. But she swivelled around to show him her ass, doing a slow 180 for him.

He licked his lips while she ushered him toward the bed.

Before she got him on the mattress, though, he put his hand on her breastbone.

She stopped breathing for a second. Now he'd go for one of her tits.

Instead, keeping one hand on her breastbone, he applied the other on her back, watching her while he pressed his hands together like he was squishing a pancake. "Oh. You'll do. I like you."

He crushed extra-hard on the word like, making her gasp, before he suddenly released her.

She fell back a step, sucking her breath in and out. He was a skinny old man, but stronger than her. He'd probably left two permanent bruises on her skin. It hurt to breathe.

Meanwhile, he clambered on the bed a little awkwardly, like her little brothers.

No. Not like her brothers. She remembered the knife.

Chapter 28

"I got to get ready," she told him, switching off the lamp beside her.

"No, I need light to film!" He sat up.

"Sorry." She turned the lamp back on, clicking it to the lowest setting, so only the area immediately around it glowed. "Striptease is better if I got more to take off. Could I grab a towel?"

He shook his head and pointed at the quilt under him.

One of her friends said that all bedspreads were covered in old cum because hotels didn't wash 'em. That was gross. But not as gross as this guy stabbing her, so ...

She grabbed the quilt and tugged with both hands. "You'll have to get off." She winked to make it sound better.

While he rolled off the other side, toward the window, the mattress sloshed underneath him.

She ripped the quilt up off of the bed and skyward. "Oh, yeah! That's beautiful!"

"Beautiful. Why are you going away?"

He'd noticed her retreating past the cart. She held the quilt up to shield herself as she rummaged in the bag for the knife.

"I'm shy. I need a little girl time," she whispered, now cursing herself for having dimmed the light. She had more shadows to hide in, but she couldn't fuckin' see the knife now. She should've left the light on, grabbed the knife, and hurried right back to his side.

"What? You going to the bathroom?"

"Maybe, in a bit," she continued in a whisper-girly voice, left hand in the air, right hand scouring the bag. Clothes. His wallet. That would be good, but she didn't have a pocket to hide it on her. "You never seen a striptease like this before."

What the hell. The knife had been on the left side of the bag. Unless he took it first somehow? Unless she saw wrong?

But her eyes were sharp. Her mom used to call her Angel, like the X Man who could see so good.

She felt a piece of wool—who needed wool right now?—and a travel kit.

Then she felt two oval pieces of metal linked together.

Handcuffs. He was going to chain her up.

29

HOPE

What do you do when your ex-beloved shows up, you find old human bones, the world's most beautiful Alien Queen messes with your brain, and your current love is obsessed with anonymous messages?

You dance.

Tucker thrashed beside me. He'd tossed his jacket and his hat on a table five minutes after Josie left, and had unbuttoned his shirt not long after.

He danced like he wanted to forget.

Griffin hung back, nodding to the beat, distracted.

Tori swayed, her eyelids shut, tilting her head up toward the disco ball that someone had hung on the ceiling.

I closed my eyes too, letting the music drift through me. Most of the time, I'm thinking, studying, talking to patients. I'm like a brain on legs. But now I was pure body.

I smiled as the music shifted to something trancelike. I could dance like this forever. Time meant nothing.

30

CLOUD

I am going to die here, *her brain said.*
No, you are not, the rest of her answered. *All you need is that goddamned knife.*

"I don't see any dancing, angel," he sing-singed.

"Just another minute, my, uh, gorgeous." *Her voice squeaked, but maybe he couldn't tell,* in a half-whisper. "I need you to lie down on that waterbed"—*the one you tried to smother me on*—"and get ready for the big show!"

"Big show."

"That's right!" *She wanted to bash his head with the pair of handcuffs.*

"You promise?"

"Oh, I promise." She peeped over the tent of the quilt and winked at him while her right hand felt a coiled rope. *How many weapons had he brought?* Her palms sweated. She hummed a random melody, raising her voice to be heard above her own heartbeat.

Then her fingers closed over a familiar plastic grip.

The knife. Covered with a sheath, but she finally held the handle in her own hand.

She started singing now, belting really, to cover the noise as she swayed back toward the bed.

He curled on the mattress like a dead bug, or a little kid. On his back, on top of the sheets, holding his knees, his eyes wide.

Was she supposed to be sexy or be his mother?

She tried for both, batting her eyelashes in a flirty way but talking sweet. "Oh, that looks nice. Why don't you get nice and warm in the electric blanket?"

He didn't say no, so first she tucked the quilt under her armpits to free her hands, then she twisted to reach for his electric blanket with her left hand.

The blanket was already warm to the touch. Looked a bit worn out too, but she ignored that as she flung the blanket open and over him as best as she could one-handed.

"Would you like me to tuck you in?"

He nodded, hypnotized, and she wrapped him as tightly as she dared, singing about moonlight the whole time. A mummy was less likely to spring at her.

She turned the blanket to its warmest setting. "There. Doesn't that feel amazing?"

"Snug," he said, in a high, soft voice.

"Yes. So snug," she agreed, gripping the knife.

31

HOPE

Someone bumped into me, and when I opened my eyes, Tucker mouthed an apology. His white hair had darkened with sweat.

Tori's slim hands steadied me, and she said something in my ear. "What?"

"Hot tub."

I stared at her and shook my head. "It's too hot!"

She winked at me, and I realized she was thinking of skinny dipping, which I'd never done in my life.

"Tori?" I mouthed at her.

She giggled and tugged on Griffin's sleeve.

32

CLOUD

Ugh. Him acting like a little kid made it harder to hate him. But she clutched the knife and smiled at him before she ducked under the quilt, so it formed a dark tent over her head. "Now, you have to trust me, that I'm going to blow your mind."

He giggled to himself. "Blow my mind?"

"Yes." She needed both hands to unsheath the knife. Weirdest knife cover she'd ever seen, with extra straps around the knife blade. Good thing that, apart from the bondage look, the clasp was just a buckle at the top of the handle. She started singing "Summertime Sadness," realized it probably wasn't a good choice for this guy, and switched back to humming to hide the sound of her opening the buckle and her kicking the sheath under the bed.

"I'm the one who'll blow your mind," he said.

Her breath hitched. Did he have a gun in that bag, too? But she clung to the knife handle and popped her head out from the quilt to wink at him. "Yeah. I bet you will."

"No." He sounded almost dreamy as he stared at the ceiling, still bundled in the blanket. "I really will. You've been so good. I'm going to give you a peek."

"Yeah?" She giggled, trying to sound like an innocent ten-year-old even though any second, he'd choke her with his dick.

Chapter 32

"Yes." He kept lying there, making no move to undo his pants. "I trust you."

"Amazing. Thanks." Her fingers curled around the knife handle. Keep trusting me.

He murmured to the ceiling, "I want you to look at what I brought on the trolley. You see how there's a cover?"

"Yes. Oh, yes, I do." If he stayed on the bed, she could grab more weapons from his bag.

"Take off the cover."

33

HOPE

Man oh man. I'd barely met Griffin, and now we might get naked in a hot tub together? Tell me that's not weird.

Luckily, I'd packed a swimsuit. They don't take up much room, and I always regret not bringing that or running shoes in case there's a gym. I wouldn't mind checking out the hot tub on the first floor.

I signalled Tori that I'd meet her there. I tapped Tucker's shoulder, but he shook his head and kept dancing. Maybe he was in the zone, or waiting for Josie, but I hollered that I was going to the hot tub and headed out the door, still moving a little to the music.

I'd have a quick dip and come back to dance some more. Who says we can't do all the things?

34

CLOUD

She held the quilt with her left hand and backed up, gripping the knife with her right. The handle slipped from her sweat.

He stayed on the bed, still curled up like a kid, and said, "It's so beautiful. Are you there yet?"

"Almost." She made sure to position herself on the knife bag side of the cart.

"Take off the cover very carefully. Do you see what I see?"

She was out of arm's reach, so she shoved the knife handle between her thighs, clutched the bedspread under her arms, and carefully slipped off the cart's cover with both hands.

He rolled on his left side in bed. She tensed and carefully took hold of the knife again, but he stayed wrapped up in the electric blanket. He only wanted to watch and instruct her from his cocoon. "Slowly. Be careful. It's an antique!"

She'd already finished revealing ... whatever this was. The cart held an old-timey looking machine with dials and wires attached to a long wooden stick.

"What do you think that is?" he asked.

Acid rose in her mouth. She swallowed it back down and whispered, "Oh, I have no clue!"

"We need two people to operate it properly. I have someone coming at 11."

Her jaw clenched. She tried not to check the time on the clock radio on the bedside table. "Really?"

"Oh, yes. Really." *His voice dropped.*

This could not be good. Add the fact that he'd been carrying it around, pushing it in front of him like a baby in a carriage? Even worse.

"Have you ever heard of Polo Lugones?"

"Gosh, no." *Could she smash this machine? If she tipped over the cart, would it break?*

But then he'd beat the hell out of her. He'd already proven that he was stronger and meaner than her. He'd packed a rope and chains and maybe a gun along with this knife.

"Push the trolley toward me. We'll be using it soon."

Her muscles locked up. No, no, no, no.

If she hesitated, would he jump out of his electric blanket and come after her?

She forced herself to steer the trolley forward, one inch at a time. She kept the bedspread in place by pressing it against her belly, protecting it from the trolley's contents. Meanwhile, her armpits were probably staining the quilt forever with her sweat.

"When I say Lugones, everyone thinks of Leopoldo Lugones, the poet and novelist. But the true genius was his son, the police chief."

She had trouble breathing now. Anybody he thought was a genius had to be off the charts.

"This instrument has a lot of advantages. It's portable, as you can see for yourself. We could use it here or in your room."

No matter how slowly she moved, she was almost right up against the bed now. But he kept talking.

"It uses a low current. That way, we can make the ... pleasure last longer." *His voice caught again.*

Oh, Christ. She gripped the knife in her right hand.

"You can apply the current where you like, and the controller changes the level of electricity."

Chapter 34

Shitfuckgoddamn.

"*Have you ever heard the quote, 'To feel the* picana *is to taste death'?*"

35

HOPE

If part of me wondered if I'd run into Ryan en route, well, yes. I'm only human. It would be just my luck to meet and greet when I was sweaty and alone.

Luckily, I managed to duck into our new room and clean up a bit before making my way down to the first floor and running into Tori on the stairs.

I'd pulled a T-shirt and shorts on over my bikini and tossed a room towel around my neck in case the hotel had run out of them at the hot tub. Tori was wearing some cute little cover up that was like a translucent white dress, sexy and demure at the same time.

She flicked the sleeve of my shirt. "Looking good."

"Yeah, right."

"Tucker will be drooling over you."

Well, that was true. And vice versa. I'm lucky that way, Ryan notwithstanding. "Like Griffin for you. You know where to go?"

"Sure. It's on the east side, in the back."

36

CLOUD

"No." She managed to push the sound out of her throat. No, she had never heard of a picana before.

"Ah. Better to experience it first hand. But of course, you must undress for the full effect. So please, carry on. You said it would be 'amazing'?"

When she'd joked about turning tricks, another girl had told her not to get in a car. "You get in, you dead," that girl said. "I don't care how much they give you. I ain't goin' in no goddamn car."

Cloud had thought a room was better than a car. Nope.

"I rented this room. No one else will disturb us except my friend. We can take all night if we want." His eyes unfocused. "You look strong. That's good."

Strong. Did he mean fat? She'd cut him extra for that one.

"I estimate we have approximately 20 minutes before my companion arrives. So please, be sure that your 'amazing' performance is at its end before then. We may need a little extra time to tune up our instrument. You see, this is truly an antique. The picana was at its peak in Argentina in the 1930's. Despite this picana's age, it is in excellent condition. I maintain it meticulously."

I bet you do, motherfucker.

His eyes hardened. "Now get dancing."

So she did. It was hard when she only had one hand, and her hand cramped and slipped around the knife.

She dragged the quilt up with her left hand, suspending it above her. She twirled to show him her ass before she spun back again. She widened her eyes, pouted her lips, dropped the bra strap off her shoulder before popping it back again.

"You're a tease. Such a little tease. I'm going to enjoy teasing you back. The picana *can give you a little hint, a little hum, of pain at first. Would you like that?"*

Hell, no. But she winked at him, rolling her shoulder, while he said, "Oh, yes, you would. I can tell. I can always pick out the right girls. The ones who struggle and scream."

Holy fuck. She should've smothered him with the electric blanket.

"And you make such sweet little sounds. You know how to cry. Pretty little tears. And almost—mewing, you know? Like a cat? No." He bared his teeth at her. "Like a precious little kitten."

Was he a serial killer? Or did he just torture girl after girl?

"I can play it for you if you like. I record every session. Video and audio. I keep a log book. I have pictures. I have everything."

She might not get out of here alive. Ever.

"I would make more money if I shared more, but I can't, because some of you have to be my pretty little secret, don't you, darling? My sweetheart."

Sorry, Mom. Guess stepdad wasn't such a fuck after all. Turns out there's worse than him. Christ. Who knew.

"Now come here."

She hammered the sweet smile on her face and held the quilt up like a shield as she lunged forward.

She might only get one hit. She had to make it count.

Maybe she shouldn't have wrapped him up in that damn electric blanket, because that was harder to cut through. At the last second, she went for his throat.

He rolled.

Fuck, he was fast. The knife plunged into the waterbed instead.

She yanked it free, ready for another go.

Chapter 36

A puddle formed behind his head and shoulder, and then he yelled and started to shake.

She jerked back, still keeping the bedspread on her, as he screamed in pain.

At first she thought he was faking it. And then, as his eyes rolled and body bucked, still screeching, she realized that he really wasn't.

37

HOPE

"How do you know your way around?" I asked Tori's back, following her down an unfamiliar set of stairs.

"We took a tour. They have hidden corridors, shelves built into walls to hide booze, and they used to have a buzzer system connected to other hotels so that if one of them got raided, they'd all get the alarm."

"Very cool."

"You should see the gambling room near the restaurant. It's disguised as a children's play room, with a chess board game built into the floor, to throw the police off their scent."

"I'll have to take the tour." I liked that she could hit the dance floor one minute, and the next, give me directions to hidden bootlegger secrets.

She stopped in front of the hot tub door, and I realized we'd come the opposite way down the hallway. Just as well, since I glimpsed someone in white disappearing the other way. I held my card above the sensor. It beeped, and Tori opened the door. Then she froze.

The good news was that the hot tub room was empty.

The bad news was that we could hear terrible noises through the plaster wall. I stiffened and bent forward, listening.

Chapter 37

"That's the honeymoon suite," said Tori.

I texted Tucker. *We need you.*

Coming, he wrote back, with a few choice emojis.

Come now.

I turned to Tori. "We can't break into the honeymoon suite. I'll call the hotel front desk."

Tori levelled her eyes at me. "You do that."

"I mean—"

Tori strode toward the wall on our right and banged on the door presumably connecting the hot tub room to the honeymoon suite. "Hello? Do you need help?" She pressed down on the doorknob's horizontal handle. Locked.

She tried her hotel card. Still locked.

I darted into the hallway. I knocked, called out, and pounded on the honeymoon suite's front door. Locked.

Someone screamed inside. I shuddered.

Tori hollered, "Call Jennifer."

First I rushed back into the hot tub room and found Tori sliding her hotel card in the crack between the door and its frame, picking the door lock.

"Tori. You can't do this." Did Tori really know how to jimmy locks, or was she only trying out of desperation?

Her jaw worked. She didn't answer.

As long as we've known each other, Tori's always been the calm, law-abiding one.

On the other hand, I haven't known Tori long. And I never asked if she could pick a door lock.

I let the woman work and called Jennifer. She'd given us her cell number, so it was less intrusive and easier than looking up the hotel number. It rang five times before Jennifer's voice recording said, "Hi, leave a message. 'Bye!"

"Jennifer, this is Hope Sze. We're in the hot tub room. Someone's screaming in the honeymoon suite. Please help. 'Bye."

Meanwhile, Tori grimaced. I heard a clunk.

"Holy shit, Tori."

She ignored me and shoved the door open.
I wasn't even sure what we saw at first.

38

There was something on the bedspread, a figure curled in a blanket.

My mouth opened in horror, just in time to inhale a weird smell wafting through the air. Like burning flesh and synthetic fabric.

Something, some*one* was on fire. I could see the open mouth and the dark eyes and bald head above the blanket.

Tori rushed toward the bed.

"No, Tori, wait!" I yelled, hitting 911. "We don't know what's going on!"

A woman's even voice answered, "911, what's your emergency?"

"I need an ambulance—" I started.

The thing on the bedspread screamed. A short, hoarse yell that choked off mid-cry.

That galvanized Tori who ran back toward the bed, her flip flops tapping on the wood floor.

"Wait, Tori. Please!"

Then Tori slipped. It happened so fast, I only had time to yell, "No!" before she hit the deck.

Her entire body spasmed.

"Tori!" I hollered.

"Why do you need an ambulance, ma'am?" the 911 operator asked.

"A man was screaming, and I think—my friend—I've got to help my friend—" I could barely get the words out.

I'd never seen anything like it. Even through her white dress, I could see her muscles clenching and relaxing and clenching again.

"Oh, my God," I realized aloud. "My friend is being electrocuted."

39

"Stay calm, ma'am," said the operator. Getting ma'am-ed in the middle of an emergency! "I'm a doctor. I have to help my friend." I surveyed the room.

King-sized bed with electrocuted human at 11 o'clock. Bedside table, 12 o'clock. Beside table, 1 o'clock. Some sort of machine at 2 o'clock. Dresser at 7 o'clock.

And right in the middle of the clock, centre-room, I spotted the puddle of water on the floor that had crept toward Tori. She'd stepped into it. Her flip flops hadn't protected her, but I was wearing sneakers. Would that be enough?

"I have to help her." I set my phone down on a chair next to the door with the operator still squawking. 911 should be able to triangulate on my location while I helped Tori.

I've never witnessed anyone getting electrocuted before. First Aid had warned me to avoid any downed power lines. Stay clear so that you don't get electrocuted yourself.

There were no downed power lines in the middle of this room. It was possible that the electric circuit for the entire room had gone on the fritz, but my mouth dried when I saw the puddle snaking from the bed toward Tori and now toward me.

Sure, I should help the person on the bed, but I only had two hands. Tori came first.

The safest thing to do was to cut the power to the entire wing. I needed the circuit breaker or a fuse box.

I checked both the hot tub room and the honeymoon suite. Nothing, which made sense. They couldn't have guests messing with the power supply, especially close to the hot tub after a few beers.

I pushed open the hot tub room door and yelled, "HELP! HELP! HELP" Then I propped that door open with one of the towels they kept on the wall, still yelling as I darted back to Tori.

She was still silently contracting. Her jaw clamped shut, and she struggled to make a sound. I imagined her agony as I yelled, "It's okay, Tori. I've got you."

Or I would soon.

My rubber soles should protect me, although I was a bit nervous relying on them alone. Rubber gloves would be better, too, right? So I didn't conduct electricity while I was moving her and end up shocked too, like a daisy chain of felled people?

"HELP! HELP!" I hollered.

"Hope?" Ryan pushed his way into the hot tub room.

Shocked yet somehow unsurprised to see him, I called, "Tori! She's getting electrocuted!"

Ryan crossed to the doorway to stare at my friend. The muscles tightened in his jaw, and he said, "I've got to cut off the power. Don't touch her."

"I have to."

"I said *don't touch her!*" Ryan sprinted into the hall, past his girlfriend, Marina.

She stopped dead. "Oh, my God."

"You have gloves?" I asked her, expecting a head shake.

She pulled a set out of her pocket. Clear, thin plastic gloves like my mom buys in bulk.

I didn't know if they'd be enough insulation, but I grabbed them anyway and held them up to the light to check for holes. It would really suck if I got electrocuted because Ryan's new girlfriend just so happened to give me hole-y gloves. But these seemed okay, if slightly large for my fingers.

Then I cautiously stepped toward Tori.

40

"What is going on here?" asked Marina as I dodged the growing puddle on the wood floor.

"Live electricity." I grimaced as my sneaker squeaked. Water silently pooled ever-closer. Where was this water coming from? What if it started to gush toward us, a tsunami of electricity?

Don't fall, don't fall.

"Ryan told you not to go in," she said.

"She's not Ryan's friend." I literally tiptoed, as if less shoe surface area contacting the floor would make the difference between me being electrocuted or not.

"It won't do either of you any good if you get electrocuted too."

"I *know* that." I gritted my teeth. Only a few more feet. I needed insulation.

Then I remembered the towel I had draped around my shoulders.

If I could have lassoed her, that would be even better. If only I had more material and expertise. I looped the towel around one of her feet and cinched it as best I could without touching Tori's skin. "Babe, I'm getting you out of here."

I yanked. That pulled the towel off her foot.

Looks easier in the movies. Firefighters have better training and equipment too.

I took one more step toward Tori, despite the water, and looped the towel again, praying that the gloves would protect me. The towel already looked damp in places.

I did my best to tie a knot. Harder than you'd think, but at least this towel had relatively long, thin material. First time in my life I'd been thankful for cheap towels.

"Come ON," I said, as I pulled again. And again.

Inch by goddamned inch.

Tori is not a big person, but neither am I. And that fucking towel started to slip off again before I got her out of the puddle.

"Got it," said Marina, coming up behind me with a long-handled wooden mop with fluorescent yellow bristles.

She moved ahead of me and placed the brush at Tori's shoulder like she'd row her in.

"On three," I called to her. "One-two-THREE!"

Together, painfully, we managed to drag Tori to the connecting door as the lights went out.

"Ryan," I said aloud. He'd found the circuit breaker.

"He saved us," she said.

"He's a superman," I agreed. "Now let's get her the fuck out of here." I nodded at the hallway, which still had the light on. Of course she probably couldn't see me, but she got my intention as I kept moving backward.

"Hope?" Tucker's voice called faintly.

"Over here!"

"Tori!" came Griffin's deeper voice.

I heard Marina gasp. She didn't want to deliver the news.

"Help!" I shouted, but we couldn't stop. We hauled Tori as best we could, pushing and pulling and bumping into stuff—I heard a clatter as something fell down, I had no idea what, but it didn't hit any of us. Made a hell of a ruckus, which was a good thing since we hadn't rung an alarm.

An alarm. Damn. I should've looked for a fire alarm. But it was already too late. We finally, with much sweat and a wrenched right shoulder from me, managed to tow Tori to the front door of the hot tub room. Hallway light spilled on us.

"What's going on?" yelled Tucker, pushing open the door for us.

Griffin didn't bother asking. With one swift move, he dragged Tori fully onto the hallway floor, bumping her head, but now he'd properly illuminated her face and chest.

She wasn't breathing.

41

I pressed Tori's carotid artery. No heart beat.
I sobbed aloud and checked the other side before starting CPR.

I have done CPR on dummies. I have done CPR on other people. But I have never pushed on a chest as fast or as hard as for Tori Yamamoto.

"Tori!" Griffin choked.

Tucker fell into place on the other side of her—body, I didn't want to say—but I didn't budge until he knelt to take over. He thumped her chest just as hard as I had.

Then I moved to her head to tilt her chin back. Her hair was silky under my hand, I realized, even as I exhaled two deep breaths into her lips.

I kissed a girl.

Her lipstick tasted sweet.

I could see her slim chest indent with the force of Tucker's contractions. "And two-and-three-and-four-and-five ... " he chanted aloud. Sweat flew off his hair and hit me.

Breathe, Tori, breathe.

I didn't care. I waited for 15 so I could give my breaths.

"I'm with 911," Ryan said, and I was grateful. Between our two calls, and this CPR, maybe Tori had a chance.

"They have a defibrillator!" Marina called, and I yelled, "Grab it!"

"I feel something," said Griffin's deep voice, and I realized he'd planted himself on Tori's other side. His big, dark hand rested on her right carotid.

"Let me feel," I told him.

He scowled at me.

"Stop CPR." I reached for her left neck, and I felt it too. A faint but unmistakeable upstroke.

"Thank God," I said, but I couldn't cry and collapse just yet. I waited for the next beat, and the next. Tori was only going about 60 beats per minute. Was that normal for her? I'd never taken Tori's pulse before.

"Sorry," I told Griffin belatedly. "If we both press on her carotid arteries, it causes a vagal reaction."

"What?" Griffin blinked from me to Tucker.

"Hope's right," Tucker said. "Both of you pressing on her carotids at the same time can slow down the heart's rate and force of contraction. You can make a healthy person faint that way. That's the last thing Tori needs."

"Hope? Are you okay? Marina?" Ryan landed beside me, and I twisted to smile at him before he scowled at me. "I told you not to touch her."

I didn't bother to answer him, either, although I heard Tucker face him. "What are *you* doing here?"

Yeah. Clusterfuck. No time for that, though. "You need to tell 911 about Tori and the other guy," I told them all.

"What other guy?" Tucker snapped.

"The guy in bed in the honeymoon suite," said Marina, and all three guys swore simultaneously. It would have been funny if it hadn't been as scary as hell.

"What on earth?" called a man down the hallway, who was

wearing black and white and looked like a waiter. I shook my head before I remembered that he could help.

"Please. My friend has been electrocuted. We need help."

Marina updated 911 while Ryan and Tucker and Griffin used their phone lights to fumble their way into the suite.

42

"The water's coming closer," I heard Tucker say.

"Stop. I don't trust the electricity," said Ryan. "If someone flips the switch again, we're all toast."

"How'd you get them to shut it off?" Griffin wanted to know, their voices growing louder as they retreated back into the hot tub room.

I squeezed my eyes shut. The bed man had stopped screaming. If a trace of current had given Tori asystole, the guy in the bed had no chance. Still, it was terrible that we couldn't even check.

"I told them it was an emergency," Ryan said.

I didn't think that was the whole story. Any wing nut can say it's an emergency. Ryan had somehow managed to convince them to shut off the electricity to these two rooms in record time.

"The water came from the waterbed," said Griffin. "How did it spring a leak? And why did it have a live current?"

"Let's move out." Ryan shrugged. My eyes followed the movement of his shoulders before I turned away. I could still hear his voice saying, "They'll figure it out. Not us."

"We'll figure it out, all right," said Tucker, handing me back my phone, and I nodded. Forget the skeleton. Who almost killed one of our best friends?

I focused on Tori instead. She lay there quietly, her chest rising and falling, and her pulse beating in her throat. "Hey. Can you hear me?"

Tori's dark eyes blinked in acknowledgement, but she didn't turn to look at me.

"I'm Hope. I'm your friend. So is Tucker. Your boyfriend Griffin is here. You know Ryan ... " *Oh, Christ. Never mind.* "Are you hurting anywhere?"

She blinked twice.

"Are you having trouble talking? You could blink once for yes, two for no. You're in pain?'

She blinked once.

She was in pain. Or I thought she was. Why couldn't she talk? Was she actually responding to me, or only blinking in confusion?

"Can you squeeze my hand?"

My phone buzzed in my pocket. Then it rang. I must've accidentally hung up on 911. Some hero I was. I let it go to voicemail.

"Tori, I'm here to help. You want to tell me where it hurts? Can you point?"

She blinked once.

I should have made yes a double blink, so I could distinguish it from a regular, my-eyes-are-dry blink. "Hang on. I want to make sure I'm understanding you. You probably have chest pain, right?"

She blinked twice.

"Um, I think you'd have chest pain because we were compressing you. Giving you CPR. I also gave you mouth to mouth before your pulse came back."

I flushed, even though it wasn't really like I'd kissed her. This was life saving.

The more important question was, did Tori understand me? Because even though I thought we'd started CPR within 4 minutes, she might have brain damage.

"We need oxygen," I said aloud. "I want to perfuse your brain. Does anyone have oxygen?"

Tucker hurried back to my side. "Hope. I called 911."

"I'm talking to them right now," said Marina, who was halfway down the hallway. "They're here. I'm going to let them in."

43

Griffin thundered into the hospital waiting room less than ten minutes after me and Tucker. We'd been carrying our car keys on us, whereas Griffin had to pop up to their new hotel room first. Which meant that Tucker was now at Tori's bedside, not Griffin.

Griffin paced back and forth in the hospital waiting room, asking me what had happened again and again.

"I'm sorry, I don't know," I told him, keeping my voice down. A little kid cradled his right elbow in the next chair, and the triage nurse was eyeballing us. "I know it doesn't make much sense. There was an electric current running through the water that came out of that waterbed. Tori tried to rescue the man in bed, and ... " I twisted my hands together.

Griffin strode toward triage. "I have to go see her!"

His raised voice got more than a few upset looks from other people in the waiting room, including a pale grandmotherly type and an elderly man holding a bloody tissue to his nose.

I spread my fingers out in front of me and patted the air, silently asking Griffin to keep his voice down. My Black friends have told me how they're not allowed to get angry in public. If Anne of Green

Gables gets angry, they make jokes about redheads. If Black men or women raise their voices, bystanders call the police because they're "aggressive."

Griffin glowered at me. "I'm her boyfriend. I should be there. You tell your guy to get out."

They would only allow one visitor at a time. Since I'd spent the most time with her so far, I'd let Tucker take a turn. But Griffin deserved face to face time with his new girlfriend.

"I will. Look, I'm doing it right now." I texted Tucker, *Please come out. Griffin's upset.*

"Of course I'm upset. Tori almost died!"

He must have amazing vision to read my text from where he stood. I tucked my phone back in my pocket. "I get that. And believe me, we did everything we could for her. I dragged her out with Marina, and Ryan cut the power, and Tucker and I did CPR."

"I know. I was there."

He had a temper. Tori hadn't mentioned that. Of course, she hadn't mentioned much of anything. I didn't want to stereotype him or doubt him, even though I was aware that he'd come into her life recently and mysteriously, possibly around the same time as my stalker.

"Sir," said the plump, fortyish blonde triage nurse from her desk, "I'm going to have to ask you to keep your voice down."

"It's fine." I flashed a plastic smile at her. "All under control."

She nodded and raised her eyebrows at me at the same time, conveying both agreement and doubt.

Griffin's fists balled, and he raised himself up to his full height. The triage nurse's eyes widened. She reached for her phone.

I inserted myself between them. "We're going for a walk. When Dr. Tucker comes out, Griffin Chao will visit instead. Okay?"

She exhaled through her nose. She was a master at expressing herself with minimal words.

I reached for Griffin's arm, but caught myself before I made contact. I didn't know him well enough to touch him.

He glared at the nurse. "I'm here to see Tori Yamamoto."

She stared right back at him. "You will as soon as we can safely let you in. Her health is our first priority."

He took a deep breath, and then I saw him flatten the fury out of his body. His shoulders lowered, his hands unclenched, and I could practically feel the relief radiating from everyone watching us in the waiting room.

Then the ER door opened, and Tucker finally walked out, his forehead creased in thought. He caught sight of Griffin and waved him in.

Griffin disappeared through the door so fast, he didn't use his hand to hold it open.

44

"What took you so long?" I whispered to Tucker after we were safely buckled in his car, me in the driver's seat. I figured I could drive and he could talk.

"I was trying to talk to her."

"Talk to Tori? And was she able to answer?" I reversed carefully, checking for any stray patients.

He shrugged and glanced out the passenger window. "Not really. But I wanted to figure out what she knew."

"About the guy in the bed?" I asked, stopping at the gate to pay for parking. It was less than 20 bucks, which was terrific for a hospital. It was easier to cover that than to figure out why Tucker was quizzing our friend who might have anoxic brain injury and/or might be intubated and unable to talk.

"Yep. Socials are on fire. Police are tight-lipped, but I hear he was looking to hire a woman to torture with whatever was in his cart. One guy swears it's a *picana*, which is some sort of cattle prod you use on humans."

That made me swear so loud that it could have created a force field around our car. "You think Tori had any more intel than that? I bet she doesn't know any more than I do."

"I also had questions about the ghost she was seeing. Griffin. Josie Tucker. But no go. They're going to observe her overnight."

"So what were you hoping to get out of her? Griffin almost got a Code White called on him, he was so raring to get to her."

"Yeah. I'm sorry about that. I couldn't help thinking about how Tori was obsessed with the Rumrunner's Rest. She researched it harder than I did. And then this whole thing about a ghost?"

"Yeah." I fell in behind one solitary car on the road. Either Windsor was a quiet town, or they'd already rushed over to the Rumrunner's Rest to gossip about the bones and dance all night.

"There's something off about the whole thing. I wondered if she was invited here too. Separately from me."

I accidentally tapped on the brakes. A black car behind us beeped, and I waved in apology as I tried to figure out the implications. "If Tori was invited separately, do you think that they set a trap for us in the hot tub room? That they lured us in and basically killed Tori?"

His mouth twisted. He reached for the radio, started to turn it on, then off again.

"You do think so!" I concentrated on stopping at the red light. I should probably pull over, I was so upset.

Tucker met my eyes this time. "I don't know anything for sure. I don't want to jump to conclusions."

"Tucker. If this was all planned, the most likely conclusion is that the stalker did this. Let's tell the police."

"Tell them what? That I got some messages on my phone, so I dragged you here and dressed up like I'm from another century?" Tucker ripped off his hat and ran his hand through his hair.

I'd forgotten he was dressed up. "People do that all the time. They know it's Rogue Con."

"I want to bring them something definitive. Something clear. Not 'I wonder if' or 'My fiancée said.'"

Stung, I said, "Your fiancée could've gotten electrocuted tonight, along with one of our best friends. They'll be looking for leads.

They'll want to know what's going on. *I* want to know what's going on."

"That's not all you want," he muttered, drumming his fingers on his window ledge.

"Hey!"

"I saw the way you looked at him." Tucker twisted to stare at me with something awfully close to hate.

I hated myself, too. This time, I did pull over to park behind a blue sedan. I hit the four-way flasher while I struggled to find the words. We both knew he was talking about Ryan. "You're right. I loved him for a long time. But I didn't touch him. I hadn't even spoken to him since we broke up. He has a new girlfriend, and you know I didn't make any secret plans to meet Ryan here because you surprised me with this trip. I promised to marry *you*."

We sat in near-silence as a white truck swept by, rumbling our vehicle.

"You didn't talk to him. But did you want to?" he asked finally.

"That's not fair. You have exes, and you're still friends with them."

He said each word as if they were stones falling out of his mouth. "But I'm not in love with them."

My heart rocketed, my cheeks burned, and I choked back tears. "I'm in love with you."

"*And* him." He bit down on the words.

I sobbed now. Not a single, noble tear, but full on eye water and snot, almost gargling with it. I did love Tucker. I didn't want to lose him. But I'd never stopped loving Ryan either, no matter how much I'd tried. Plus Tori had technically died, her boyfriend was a bit wild, and my stalker had probably orchestrated this entire debacle. For what? Why?

Then I blew my nose and started crying over Tucker all over again.

I'm going to lose Tucker. I never deserved him. Ryan will keep fucking Asian Barbie, and I'll be alone.

A cyclist clanged his bell as he passed us.

I raised my head. When I finally smeared the tears out of my eyes, Tucker sat quietly beside me, looking out the window.

"This is the stalker's fault," I told him. "He wants us to fight. Ryan was out of the picture, and I won't see Ryan again, probably ever in my life. I love *you*. Please."

He sighed and finally turned toward me. His eyes were shiny and bloodshot even under the yellow light of the street lamp. Seeing his beautiful face squeezed my heart. I loved this guy more than the sky.

Love me. Keep loving me, even though I'm so fucked up.

"If it's the stalker, he's only showing me what I already knew," he told me.

"No."

"It's my own fault. I wanted you so much, I was willing to do anything for you. Including ignoring who you really wanted." He smiled crookedly at me. "It's okay."

"NO. Tucker. I can change. I just need time. Ryan and I broke up what, four months ago? After *four years*." I sobbed so hard, he might not understand a word. "It'll take me a while to work through it, but I. Love. You. Please. Give me another chance."

He reached forward and touched my face. "The hell of it is, I understand it. Even if I find someone else, I'll always be a sucker for you."

Since I couldn't stop crying, he sighed and said, "C'mon, babe. Let's go crash. I'll drive."

The rest of the drive to the hotel was a blur. I kept talking to him, telling him that this was the stalker, that's all. *Don't let the stalker play head games. We're not breaking up, right?*

Right?

He signalled left and turned into the parking lot without answering.

"Tucker. I'm not getting out of this car before you talk to me."

"What's the point of talking?" he asked. "Those are just words."

I couldn't argue that point, but I wanted to scream. "We're being manipulated. If I hadn't seen Ryan, I would eventually have—well, not forgotten about him, but let him go. The stalker pushed us in each other's faces on purpose. It's all a game, Tucker. Come *on*."

He turned his brown eyes straight on me. "Maybe you're right. But I can't handle the game anymore."

"Don't let him win!"

He reached for the door handle. I hit the universal door lock on my side, but I was too late, and anyway, it would only have delayed him for a second before he unlocked it.

If he wanted to go, I couldn't stop him.

He stood with the door open. Rain sprayed sideways, hitting his back with a few drops on me, but neither of us cared. He bent his white head into the car and spoke directly into my face.

"I'm not letting him win. I'm taking a break."

"What does that mean?"

"It means I'm not going to fight about this. I'm going to interview Josie now."

"Josie?"

"Yeah. I have to unravel what happened to White Lightning. Is he really related to us? And what about the chimneysweep angle? Does it have something to do with the bones in the chimney?"

That *was more important to him? Bones and Josie instead of me and him?* I thought, but didn't say aloud.

"No," he said, as if he could hear me, "that stuff doesn't really matter. But it's something I might be able to fix, goddamnit."

He slammed the door closed, hard enough to rock the car.

Then he set out in the rain. I tracked his white hair through the windshield.

If I was right, and this was the stalker's doing, that bastard was a brilliant tactician.

He'd stopped Tori's heart, moved Griffin to her side at a hospital where they might call the police on him, and smashed up me and Tucker.

I was alone. And I'd cry more over that pretty damn soon.

But Tucker was right that I could solve one thing. I could identify this motherfucking stalker and throw him behind bars.

Once I did that, and Ryan voluntarily withdrew from my life, my heart would switch over to monogamy. Eventually. Widows and widowers did that all the time.

I watched the rain fall through the car windshield. The window fogged up from my breath. Police cars filled every remaining space in the parking lot, and now a cop was posted at the front door. He'd want to see proof that I was staying here. Maybe they'd interview me some more.

I pocketed my keys, and the sound of them clinking together rang in the night. One key was for our shared apartment. One was for my car, one was for his, and one was for my family's front door. Tucker and I were still linked together, our relationship cast in metal, but I couldn't stop thinking of the unnaturally calm look on Tucker's face when he walked away from me.

Then I wrote on the windshield condensation with my index finger, carefully tracing each letter backwards so that the stalker could read it from the outside if he was watching me and gloating.

ИЯUT YM

45

My phone rang. I glanced down at the screen, and my belly clenched.
Ryan Wu

I took a deep breath and pressed the green button. "Hi, Ryan."

"Hi. You okay?"

I swallowed hard. "Yup. You?"

"Yep. That was pretty amazing."

I closed my eyes and forced myself to say, "Yeah, Marina was ... a trooper."

He paused. Did I detect a sigh? Before I could get too worked up, he said, "Yeah. So let me tell you what I saw just now."

"Okay." My voice cracked. *Smooth, Hope. Real smooth.*

"Yeah." I heard a thread of amusement in his voice, and my mouth twitched too before he said seriously, "A girl ran down the hall."

I tried to compute. "A little girl?"

"No. The one with the cotton balls. She almost knocked me down. Didn't you see someone in white running from the honeymoon suite?"

I knew what he was telling me. "Cotton Ball Girl was with the combover guy."

"Yep. And although the police are keeping it quiet, Marina heard that he had a torture device on that cart."

I swore quietly to myself. Normally Ryan hates cursing, but this time, he said, "Right there with you."

"He was torturing her, and she managed to escape." I rubbed my forehead, trying to think. "We saw her running away, but maybe she went back to the scene of the crime, or never got very far, especially with all the cops. Which way was she going?"

"That's the funny part. She was running back down to the basement."

"The basement," I repeated.

"Yep."

"Where we found the bones."

He didn't answer. He didn't have to.

"I'm going to the basement," I said.

"I'm coming with you."

46

I didn't trust myself alone with Ryan. I called Tucker while I stared at the rain drops splotching the windshield.

His muffled voice answered. "I'm waiting to talk to the police, Hope. They want to talk to you too. I said I'd send you to the front desk."

"Oh." We'd already spoken to the police at the hospital.

"And as soon as they let me go, Josie's meeting me."

"Seriously?" She was still awake?

"Yeah. I'm so close to figuring it out, Hope. I think she has the final clue."

I ground my teeth as rain hammered the car roof. "Okay. Well, I'll head down to the basement with Ryan."

"You'll *what?*" His voice sharpened.

"Yep. I can't help Tori any more, but I can help that girl with the cotton balls. Ryan's the one who told me about it, so he's in." I smacked the steering wheel for emphasis.

"You're going to help the girl. The girl you think might have killed the guy in the bed."

"Wouldn't you?" My blood pulsed even contemplating Combover

Guy, let alone the possibility of getting locked in a room with him and his cattle prod.

"No. I'd go to the police."

I sighed. "Really? That's what you would do, even if you were a woman or BIPOC?" He knew as well as I did that justice wasn't usually served as neatly if you were poor, female, or Black/indigenous/a person of colour.

"I think so." But his voice was more subdued. "Okay, I'll meet you down there."

I already regretted calling Tucker. He didn't get it. This could be disastrous. But I couldn't un-call him, so I said, "Okay."

47

CLOUD

Anything gets fucked up, meet me in the basement.
That's what J told her. So that was what she had to do.
She'd hidden in a hall closet until she calmed down, which took ... an hour? More? She'd lost track of time. The one good thing about this hotel was tons of hiding places. When she remembered J's advice, she'd tiptoed downstairs. She had no shoes, but J would have dozens. J would save her.

She'd barely cleared the stairs before she saw the back of a bunch of Rogues pointing and taking pictures of yellow police tape marking off the scene.

No cops, at least none that she saw, but she plastered herself against the wall and tried to breathe.

The bones. How could she forget the bones?

A man seemed to hear her. He turned and stared directly at her, his creepy white mask shining in the dim light.

She turned away, but she could still feel that man's eyes on her.

Okay. She had no phone and the basement was off-limits. She didn't feel safe. What if the cops came crawling around? What if that mask man started following her?

The mask man lifted his right arm, showing her his silver crossbow.

Chapter 47

She dashed back up the stairs, trying not to scream. Maybe she should get out of the hotel. But when she tiptoed toward the closest exit, a cop was screening everyone.

She was trapped.

She needed clothes. J had helped her glue the cotton balls on and explained her character to everyone who asked. But right now, she needed to blend in. Everyone would remember this outfit. It was like wearing an orange jumpsuit if she headed out there.

So she had to steal clothes. And a phone if she could.

She felt bad about it, but she'd already probably killed a guy, so ...

She hurried back up to the dance party on the top floor.

Drunk people, dark place. Good place to steal.

Except she stood out in her white bra and panties, white skin, and light hair.

She skirted the edges. It was late enough and hot enough that people had kicked off their costumes.

She found a black shirt wadded in the corner and threw it on. It was five sizes too big, which was good. She could wear it as a dress. It was sticky and stinky with damp sweat and overheated deodorant, but she thought of the man on the bed and had no more fucks to give. She'd wear shit and puke if it got her out of here.

She found lots of shoes too, either costume shoes or high heels. Those were no good. She kept going and found a pair of running shoes covered in pink glitter.

She wasn't crazy about the colour—she wanted to disappear—but they looked about her size, and they were partly smeared with dirt. Maybe whoever owned these wouldn't miss them too much.

Shoes on, she headed for the front door, trying not to run, trying not to attract attention, but a man stopped her.

The blue man, the one with makeup all over his body blocked her with an outstretched arm. "You okay? You need me to order an angel shot?"

She stared at him in confusion. She tried to remember what J said, about being sexy around guys, but all she could do was smile and nod.

"Okay," he said. He dropped his arm, and she ran.

48

HOPE

Ryan and I checked the cordoned-off basement before moving up to the attic bar. It was less crowded now, which was good in that we might be able to find her, but after fifteen minutes, neither of us had sighted a single cotton ball, so I started quizzing people.

Some of them were seriously lit. They either laughed at me or stared past me. A half-dozen of them had fallen asleep near the bathroom, so I ignored those. Low yield. They were probably asleep when Cotton Ball Girl went by too.

The music was so loud that I wrote "Have you seen the girl wearing cotton balls?" in a huge font on my phone, waved to attract people's attention, and shoved the screen in their faces.

Then I remembered that I'd taken some pictures. Sure enough, one of them showed Cotton Ball Girl, albeit somewhat blurry when I cropped it. Still better than asking people manually. I added HAVE YOU SEEN HER? at the bottom and flashed that at anyone conscious.

"No way, man!"

"No, ma'am."

Ma'am-ed again. One skinny, pimpled white guy laughed crazily when I held up the pic. "I'll do her if you got her!"

Chapter 48

I glowered at him, but he held up two fingers in the peace sign before knocking back a shot.

I took a picture of his back. It turned out blurry, but at least I captured his red T-shirt with the number 9 on the back. Maybe that would come in handy.

I headed toward the hall. My ears felt irritated by the music, and sweat lay in a damp layer on my skin. I don't normally sweat much, but this was an enclosed space with too many people.

"I know you," said a man's voice.

I glanced over my shoulder at a 60 year old white man, maybe five foot eight, with brown hair and a moustache. No obvious costume. An unremarkable guy.

But anyone could be my stalker. Especially someone who didn't stand out, but who made a point of interacting with me.

"Hi, have we met?" I said, with a professional smile. It was also possible he'd been my patient.

"Hello, Hope."

I maintained my grin, although it was more defensive than genuine. "Hello."

"How are you doing?"

"Busy. Have you seen this woman?" I showed him the phone.

He took my phone and held it gently in both his hands. I got the strange feeling that he was caressing it. "Oh, yes."

"When?"

A faint smile crossed his mouth. He had even, white teeth so bleached that they looked fake. "She could tell you." He pointed at a woman down the hall with red pigtails sticking straight out from her head. I thought maybe she was supposed to be Pippi Longstocking, whom I wouldn't have called a villain, but definitely a rogue. Pippi even had a monkey on her shoulder.

"Thank you," I said, although my tone was anything but grateful. "Could you remind me how we met?"

"I'm sorry I'm so forgettable," he replied.

"Not at all. I'd like to renew our acquaintance. How did we meet?"

"I came to Rogue Con."

"I can see that." I cudgelled my brain, to quote a book I'd read in middle school (it means thinking hard). I couldn't remember talking to him. Maybe he was one of the background guys at the bar when we first arrived. Maybe he'd come to gawk at the bones. Maybe he'd goggled at the queen.

He bowed at me and left.

I frowned. Was he my stalker? Or some rando who wanted to help?

I didn't have time to worry, although I filed his face away. Brown eyes, receding brown hair, eyes slightly close together, nose a touch long, bleached teeth.

"Have you seen the girl wearing cotton balls?" I asked Pippi Longstocking, as Ryan rejoined me.

"What's she supposed to be?"

Ryan understood before I did. "I think maybe Tomura Shigaraki, but it could be anyone."

She nodded and took a closer look at the picture. "Ohhh, yeah. I saw her with Jazz. The alien queen," she added when I looked confused.

The queen. My stomach squeezed. I wanted to see her again, but I needed to fit the pieces together. "With the guy who was giving her flowers?" The combover guy, I realized. Maybe that's when he noticed Cotton Ball Girl. He was bowing toward the alien queen, and then he ended up fixating on the vulnerable human next to him.

"The flower guy followed the litter. The three of them headed out together."

So. The Combover Guy, Cotton Ball Girl, and the Queen headed out of a bar together. Then Combover Guy ended up dead and Cotton Ball Girl fled.

"Where is the queen?" I asked.

She smiled. "In her chamber."

"Which one is hers?" I knew it wasn't our room, Tori's room, or the honeymoon suite, but that still left at least ten rooms.

Pippi touched one of her pigtails instead of answering. I wasn't

Chapter 48

sure if that was a clue—the left pigtail, meaning that her room was on the left of the building?

Then Ryan handed her some folded bills, which Pippi graciously accepted before she said, "I'll bring you over. Otherwise, you wouldn't be allowed in."

I frowned at Ryan on the way over. How had he known to bribe her? Why am I always missing cues like that? She would have had to hold out her hand with her palm up, fingers beckoning, before I figured that out.

He shrugged and gestured at me to follow Pippi down to the main entrance. Wait, what? She wanted to leave the building?

A male police officer stopped us. "We don't want people coming in and out of the building."

Pippi smiled at the officer and held up a pack of cigarettes.

"It'll give you cancer," the cop said, but he smiled at her.

"Promise?" She winked at him and headed into the rain, cocking her hip.

After a beat, I followed her. Ryan took off his jacket and held it over my head. It meant he got soaked within seconds. It was one of the courtly things he always did without being asked. One of the things I loved about him. Tucker could be extremely romantic ... or he might forget that I existed if he was learning a magic trick or mastering a new language with one of his bros.

I mouthed a thank you, and Ryan smiled back at me even though his hair was already plastered against his forehead and rain dripped in his eyes.

Then we both followed Pippi, who had whipped a tiny umbrella out of her skirt somehow. She kept it over her own head, which meant that raindrops fell on the stuffed monkey around her neck, but she ignored that and beckoned us toward a trailer parked in the last row.

She knocked on the trailer door in a complicated pattern that varied in speed and rhythm before ending in three sharp knocks.

The door opened, revealing a Latinx-looking guy who eyeballed her until she passed over some of Ryan's cash and murmured a few words in his ear.

He jumped off the steps, holding the door open. Pippi curtseyed and gestured at both of us to go in.

I glanced at Ryan's unsettled expression and said, "Can't be worse than the honeymoon suite. Someone in white literally ran away from that one." I climbed up the trailer's three metal steps. The door looked like an open black mouth. I winced and started to reach for Ryan's hand.

But I remembered Tori's still body, her heart that we had to pound back to life. My arms still ached faintly from doing CPR, my shoulder too.

And I stepped into the trailer, although I lingered so I could feel the warmth of Ryan's presence at my back.

The guard kept the door open until we both entered. Then he shut it behind us while he and Pippi remained outside.

49

I couldn't see a thing inside the darkened trailer, although I could hear my own breath, and Ryan's behind me.

Part of me screamed. We could easily die in this tin can of a room. Walked into—no, even paid for—the privilege of this trap.

My heart banged so hard that I gritted my teeth, afraid that if I opened my mouth, it might fly out.

I know that's anatomically impossible, but fear spiked in my belly. I could smell my own sweat, and our wet hair and clothes, and earth.

If the stalker had lured me here, he'd done an excellent job.

But I wasn't going to scream. I wasn't going to beg. I'd let this play out.

As long as we stayed by the thin aluminum door. If the guard tried to hold it closed, Ryan and I should be able to bust it down between the two of us.

Ryan's presence calmed me. Rooted me. Even if I never saw him again after this night, he was standing by me one final time, and I loved him even more for it.

I peered into the darkness. I'm super near-sighted from genetics plus constantly hitting the books, but the advantage is that I'm not as scared when I have to rely on my other senses.

I smelled something new: a deep, dark perfume, full of musk.

I couldn't feel or taste anything, which was a bonus because this was starting to remind me of the world's worst haunted house ride.

I tuned into my ears.

It was dark, but I could hear a third person's long, slow inhalations and exhalations. Not the sucking Darth Vader sound, but something even more primordial.

My heart thundered. I snarled, cutting through the silence. "I'm not here for games. Do you have that girl?"

Something flashed in the the dark at the back of the trailer.

My first thought was of a weapon, and I tensed.

No. They'd turned on a screen.

The sound of an accordion trilled, and to my astonishment, I recognized the cheery video: "Be Our guest," from Beauty and the Beast.

Okay. That was trippy, but we were this person's guest, involuntarily, so I watched for the few seconds until it dissolved and The Phantom of the Opera sang from the depths of his opera house, his pale mask illuminated in the dark.

I heard Ryan's quick intake of breath behind me. He'd sung "The Music of the Night" at a youth group talent show years ago. Could my stalker have figured this out? But the song wouldn't necessarily mean anything to Tucker. Could the stalker have engineered me and Ryan coming here together? How?

Next, a small white bird with a grey head and grey wings chirped.

"That's a mockingbird," said Ryan.

How he knew that, I had no idea, but I was impressed even as the mockingbird began to squawk.

Was this video telling us where to find Cotton Ball Girl, or was it 100 percent mind games?

I spoke into the darkness. "Are you Jazz? Otherwise, we're leaving."

The video returned to blackness.

"Okay, 'bye." I faced the door and poked Ryan to back up.

He didn't budge. He wanted to decode whatever they'd set in front of us.

"I'm not playing this game," I told him. "I'm here to help someone in need. I refuse to get sidelined."

I could feel the tension in Ryan's back. He didn't want me to piss off the video mastermind in case we missed a clue.

Screw it. I pushed past Ryan, who slowly pivoted to let me go, and rattled the screen door. The guard had locked it.

I fumbled with the door handle, searching blindly for a lock, before I banged the door on its frame hard enough for us all to feel the vibration through our feet. "Let me out or I will break myself out."

Out of the darkness came a woman's voice. "Hope."

I pivoted around to see who spoke.

My name had actually come from the stereo speakers, accompanying a brand new video. I watched a whole series of people saying or speaking the word hope. I recognized everyone from Barak Obama to Ted Lasso to Winona Oak and the Chainsmokers

Goosebumps prickled my arms. "Let me the fuck out of here." I reared back to kick the door when a live woman's voice cut in. "Hope."

A low, sultry voice. A sex voice that made my breath catch and my nipples stand at attention.

What the ...

Ryan swore quietly behind me. He'd been affected too. Which satisfied me in a low brutal way. Marina didn't completely own him if another woman's voice could make him hard with a single syllable.

Of course this wasn't only a woman. This was the next thing to a goddess, saying, "Please don't go. I'll tell you what you need to know."

If the sound of my name alone thrilled me, her promise kept me spellbound. She seemed like the embodiment of the legendary sirens who drove men mad, making them crash their ships into the rocks. I understood them deep in my bones.

No. I shook my head and bounced up and down on my toes, working out my fingers and chanting, "Celery stalk, celery stalker," to remind myself who had sent this woman, if she wasn't the stalker herself. I felt Ryan's confusion behind me, but I couldn't worry about that right now.

I couldn't stop up my ears with wax like Odysseus, but I could distract myself.

She snapped on lights facing me and Ryan. White light dazzled my retinas. I squeezed my eyelids shut, shaded my orbits for good measure, and told her, "Fantastic. Tell me how to find the girl who ran out of the honeymoon suite before us."

"Ah. Do you know who she is?"

"Do you?" I countered.

She paused. "You're so strategic, Hope. I appreciate your thinking. But you see, I am the one holding the strings here. Answer my question."

Her voice still enthralled me, but she seemed a touch self-satisfied. I clung to that chip in her perfection. "I don't know her name. I can send you a photo." That felt like a betrayal, but I'd shown it to others. Why should Jazz be any different?

My fingers hesitated. I didn't want to hand her my phone number. Although I block my caller ID, whoever bugged our room could probably break that within seconds.

"Wonderful," she purred.

My phone buzzed, and I received a text from JB: *Give it to me.*

I sucked my breath between my teeth. She knew the sexual effect she had on everyone post-puberty. She capitalized on it while neatly demonstrating that she already had my contact information.

I texted back the photo.

She burst out laughing. "Hope. I admire the effort, I really do, but how many people would recognize her from this?"

"Her costume was memorable," said Ryan.

"It certainly is, Ryan Wu. How *delicious* to hear from you."

Ryan turned silent. I knew, without being able to see him, that he must be blushing.

"How many men, or women, can resist a young fawn like Cloud?" she asked.

I shook my head. The woman in front of us attracted me far more than a mostly-naked girl, even though I'd never seen Jazz's face.

"See how slender, how innocent, how potentially helpless she is," Jazz continued.

Ryan cut in gruffly. "We're here to *help* Cloud."

She chuckled. "That's what you all say."

I took over. Good cop, B&D cop. "Look. You seem to be implying that we want her for ... carnal reasons."

She gave a full-throated laugh.

I ignored that."That's not it at all. We want to make sure she's safe."

"Safe from what, dear heart?"

My heart leapt involuntarily from even a fake endearment. I swallowed, willing away the heat in my cheeks, still masking my eyes and maybe my embarrassment. "She escaped from the honeymoon suite where a man was electrocuted. The first thing is to make sure that she's medically stable. You can appear normal and collapse later."

She sounded distinctly amused. "We can observe her for you, if that's what you're asking."

"Who's we?" I rapped out.

"I can't grant you an answer so lightly, Hope. You'll have to do better than that."

"Define better." Even though my stomach flip flopped like a sunfish on land when she said my name.

"Show me how much you know, and I'll reward you with additional knowledge. It's a cycle of positive virtue." Sarcasm edged in her voice. Was she the stalker, or was she quoting him?

Either way, I needed to shut down this cat and mouse game. "I believe this entire weekend was orchestrated by my stalker." Ryan sucked in his breath behind me, but I continued, "He approached Tucker and probably Tori. They became enamoured with a mystery at the Rumrunner's Rest and brought me and Griffin here." I hesitated.

"Darling, you're forgetting someone. What about Ryan?" she asked.

Ryan stirred behind me, but he didn't speak.

"His new girlfriend received the blueprints for the Rumrunner's Rest. Ryan figured out that there was something behind the chimney. Somehow, she got permission to open it up and turn it into a media event, on the same weekend that Tucker brought us here."

"All for your benefit? Hope, you do think highly of yourself, don't you," Jazz said.

"I do. But that's not why. As Sherlock Holmes said, 'Once you've eliminated everything else, you must consider the impossible.'"

She tinkled another laugh. "How on earth does your soap opera relate to Cloud?"

"I don't know," I told the darkness. "I have no clue why he'd get off on endangering a young woman I've never met before. But she may have been used as bait for me and Tori. We did find her, even if Tori was hurt."

"More than hurt, I'd say. The poor thing nearly died," said Jazz.

Ryan exhaled behind me.

I jerked up to my full height and stabbed my finger in Jazz's direction. "Yes. He almost took out one of my best friends. But we got her back."

"Arrived too late to save the man in bed, didn't you?"

My nails cut into my own palms. "Yes."

"How do you feel about that?"

It's a medical school question. *How did that make you feel?*

"It was too bad," I said.

"No, no, no, Dr. Sze, that's not a proper answer. How did it make. You. Feel?"

I didn't want to answer with Ryan behind me. I already came off as a bitchy robot compared to the sensitive, charitable, God-loving women who fluttered around him at church.

But Jazz must have an excellent B.S. detector, and she was the one I needed to please right this second. "I try to save everyone. I haven't had a chance to really think about him yet, though, between running to the hospital and back." And Tucker breaking up with me, but no need to disclose that little morsel. "Frankly, if he was a bad guy, I'm not going to waste too many tears on him."

Jazz tapped her hands together in the darkness. Clap. Clap. Clap. Clap.

I gritted my teeth. Slow clapping can be a compliment, or it can be sarcastic.

Ryan rested his hand on my shoulder. He didn't say anything, but my eyes prickled with tears, savouring the fact that he was voluntarily touching me for the first time in months.

Then his hand fell back down to his side.

I kept my posture still, refusing to waver, even though that quick withdrawal was a gut punch. Any percentage of Ryan I got tonight was temporary and forbidden.

Jazz's dazzling voice took over again. "One thing we've always admired is your honesty, Hope. What if I told you that he was indeed a bad guy? One of the worst guys? And that it's a good thing he's gone?"

"I would ask for proof that he was a bad guy. Then I'd give it to the police."

"Oh, Hope. You always ask for so much."

"No, I asked you for the minimum. Tell me where Cloud is so that I can make sure she's safe. If you want to throw in bonus evidence that a bad guy went down, I'll take it. Especially if my stalker is willing to lay off afterward."

"It's a good thing that you're so lightly amusing."

That was the last thing I would have called myself, but whatevs. As long as she told me what I wanted. I waited, ideally amusingly.

"Very well," she said. "We will send some information along."

I waited for more. I'd given her everything I had. What else could I do to make her give me Cloud's location?

Ryan laid it all out. "What about Cloud?"

"You can find her."

"Are you giving us more clues?" he asked.

"Yes, grasshopper." I could hear the smile in Jazz's voice.

The flatscreen TV illuminated once more. Before she shut off the bright lights, I caught a glimpse of a slim figure to the right of the screen.

A dark-haired anime character popped onto the screen, in a cartoon meadow. She wore clouds around her breasts and nether regions, so I could see how Cloud had either approximated this character's costume, or they'd made an avatar to look like her, except as a brunette.

Cartoon Cloud's mouth moved, but I didn't hear anything as she moved from the meadow into a house.

"Can you turn the sound on?" I asked.

Jazz laughed. The volume bar, set at maximum, appeared in the screen's right hand corner, but no speech emerged. This was a silent movie.

A bald cartoon character crept into the meadow as raindrops pattered on his head.

Hmm. He didn't have a combover, but the lack of hair and his hunched posture was enough to give me pause.

A bolt of lightning struck the bald guy on the head. He sizzled, heat radiating from his body, before he turned into a tall, black lump of coal that tipped face first.

Cartoon Cloud rushed out the door, but instead of heading for the meadow, she climbed up the side of the house to the roof.

I frowned. The attic bar was stuffed with Rogues. The police stood guard at each exit. But what if Cloud climbed past all of them and onto the roof?

50

The peaked summit of a building seemed like the worst place I could imagine during a rainstorm.

On the other hand, Cloud wouldn't be thinking too clearly. And maybe the stalker had forced her up there.

After endless jerking around, did Jazz hand us the answer: find Cloud on the Rumrunner's rooftop?

"Thank you," I managed to squeeze out of my throat. Even though Jazz was either my stalker or a representative thereof, she'd upheld her half of the bargain.

Ryan reached for the trailer's door first.

This time, it opened. When we stepped out, both Pippi and the guard had melted into the night, but rain drops plopped eagerly on my head.

My kingdom for a windbreaker. No time for that, either. I shoved my wet bangs out of my face.

"The roof," I told Ryan.

He frowned before spreading his jacket over both of our heads. "I don't know if we should take the cartoon literally. When you think about it, it's pretty much impossible that they could have rigged up an animation in the time since she disappeared, unless they'd planned—"

"The roof," I repeated. "It's our only lead. Find me the easiest way to get up on the roof. If you don't, Jennifer will." I reached for my phone.

Ryan held up his hands in surrender, and I pocketed my phone. I didn't want it to get wet anyway.

We jogged through the wet parking lot. When we arrived at the Rumrunner's door, Kathy and Joan were arguing with the police officer, telling him that they needed something from their car. Ryan and I managed to slip in by explaining that we were here to talk to the police.

Technically true. I failed to mention that we'd talk to them later.

"We should have taken the tunnel," said Ryan.

"What tunnel?"

He waved his hand. "Marina and I haven't checked it out yet. I don't know how safe it is. But there's a tunnel from the basement that leads to the river and maybe even underneath it."

"Maybe Cloud went that way." But I imagined crawling into a century-old, eroded dirt tunnel, with the weight of a polluted river above us, and shuddered.

He nodded. "Let's do the roof first and make sure she's not there. According to the blueprints, there's a back way out of the attic bar."

"Show me."

He led me up the stairs, but instead of turning right toward the attic bar, he ran his hand along the opposite wall. After he found the seam he wanted, he pulled out a pocket knife and stuck the blade into the seam to open a latch.

I goggled at him, but he didn't wait for applause. He pivoted that section of wall toward us and motioned me into a narrow hallway papered with newspapers.

I glanced over my shoulder to make sure no one else noticed me slipping inside. I turned on the flashlight on my phone, advancing a few steps so Ryan could join me and pull the wall closed behind us.

The hall was a foot wide, maybe less. "Should I keep walking?" I whispered.

"Let me go ahead of you so I can find the door." He angled himself sideways. I pressed myself against the wall and held my breath, but he couldn't help brushing his back against my front.

On top of everything else, he smelled good. Like soap and maybe a faint cologne and his own sweat. I inhaled him after he passed, hoping he didn't notice.

"It's not far," Ryan muttered, and I nodded, red-faced, even though he couldn't see me behind him.

Ten feet through the jagged passage, he popped open another secret compartment in the wall. It held a sturdy wooden crate that he pulled out to step on. The crate had been smudged by hands and shoes, but it didn't look a hundred years old. People had come here more recently.

Ryan stretched his hand skyward.

I shone the light up. "Holy—"

We both stared at the trap door faintly outlined in the ceiling.

"How do you know all this? Is this part of the tour?" I whispered, angling my light toward his hands as he reached for the trap door.

He braced one hand against the ceiling and used the other to tug out a latch he'd secreted out of the door face itself.

I raised my eyebrows. "Is this seriously on the blueprints?"

"She has two sets of blueprints, the official ones and the unofficial ones."

"How'd she get the unofficial ones?"

He grunted and began to pull the trap door toward us. Dust fell on both of us, smarting my eyes. I belatedly bent over to protect them.

"She bought into it," he said. "She's a part owner of this place."

"What?"

As if in answer, something nearly smacked us in the head. I felt it whip by my face as I shielded my still-teary eyes and stifled a shriek.

Ryan showed me that he'd caught a rope ladder. "It's supposed to be attached here," he murmured, re-hooking the ladder on the upper side of the door that would have made the floor of the secret room above us.

That made me think we were following in Cloud's tracks. She'd managed to get up here, but had dislodged the rope ladder in her haste.

"Ladies first," said Ryan, stretching the rope ladder out in front of me, and I started climbing. I hated the way each rope step sagged under my feet, and the feel of the rope rasping against my palms, but it wasn't a big climb. Within minutes, I stepped into another little room with a faded checkerboard pattern of black and white squares painted onto the floor.

"They have a children's playroom on the ground floor too," said Ryan, stepping beside me and coiling up the rope ladder. "Of course they were actually gambling in both rooms."

I gulped as I shone my phone flashlight around the room. Dozens of porcelain dolls filled the rows of a bookshelf, staring at me with their long-lashed blue eyes, displaying their faded white dresses. A stuffed clown with harlequin markings around its eyes sat on the end of the first row. A jack in the box grinned at us, having sprung free long ago.

Music drifted toward us from the ball downstairs, which made it more creepy instead of less.

Ryan ignored it all as he shut the trap door. Still more dust flew in the air. "The roof door was a last ditch escape during the police raid. They could step out on the roof—the escape door is only about a foot off the floor—and wait on a ledge. There are even hand-holds on the roof if you look close enough."

He stuck his knife into the frame beside the creepy doll shelf. That popped the latch allowing him to spin the shelf into the room. Then he unsealed another door on the other side, with minimal ceremony.

How had he known all this? It wouldn't be on the blueprints. Those might show extra rooms, but not exactly how to find your way into them.

No time to ask. The escape door was tiny, forcing even me to crouch as I followed Ryan up the narrowest set of stairs that creaked under our feet, barely illuminated by our phones. I had the feeling that we'd crawled into the very walls of the house, which made me think of the chimney bones.

I shivered. Above us and beside us, rain slammed the roof relentlessly.

"Do you really want to do this?" Ryan asked.

"I know it's raining. I know it's stupid. But if that video told us this was where to find Cloud, and we didn't check it out, I'd never forgive myself."

He nodded in agreement, threw a lock, twisted a knob I couldn't see, and shoved open the final door.

That was the idea, anyway.

The door didn't stir.

Ryan frowned and put his shoulder into it. The wood began to move.

Faintly, through the roof and the spatter of rain, I heard a girl scream.

51

"Cloud?" I called.
No answer.
Tonight was my night for talking to females I couldn't see. "Cloud, my name is Hope. I'm here to help you. I have a friend with me, Ryan."

She sobbed. I couldn't make out any words.

"Please, Cloud. Let us help you." I wasn't 100 percent sure it was Cloud, but between the cartoon and her limited reaction, I'd bet on it. "It's not safe on the roof. Please come in." She might be standing on the ledge, but it could give way, especially in an icy climate like ours.

"No!"

Ryan and I exchanged a look. We both heard that one.

"The roof is slippery," I said. "It's raining. Come in, and you'll be safe and warm."

"No!"

"Okay. I understand." She was responsible for a man's death, and police stood guard around the building.

I waited. No response. She was listening, though, so I continued. "We know what happened, and we—I—don't blame you. Come inside."

She started crying again.

Poor little bird. How old was she? Once I got into my 20s, I lost the ability to stratify teenagers by year, but I'd guess maybe 15. She was so young and vulnerable, nearly naked and sent to do whatever a terrible man wanted. Then she'd killed that torturer. What was her ACEs (Adverse Childhood Experiences) score now?

"Cloud. We're not the police. We want to help you."

She called something out to the wind and rain. I caught the end: " ... I'm dead."

"No. You're still alive. Listen. Do you have any family or friends I can call?"

Only the rain answered me. I moved on. "Could I call—" Suddenly, it came to me—"Jennifer, who works here? She fights human trafficking. She might be able to help you." It was a far cry from fundraising to hands-on helping a girl on the rooftop of your building, but I was desperate. Sweat stung my hairline.

Cloud stayed silent. But she hadn't said no. That was a step forward, right?

"You probably met Jennifer before. She was in the bar. She has long, brown hair and freckles. Super nice person. She'll understand." *I hope.*

"We all think that what happened to you was wrong," Ryan said.

"Who's that?" Cloud almost screamed.

I tensed. Ryan snapped his mouth shut, and I tried my most soothing voice. "That's Ryan. He's the one who opened up the chimney tonight, with his girlfriend." Saying that literally gave me stabbing chest pain. I couldn't bring myself to add Marina's name. Fuck her. No, not that way. "He's on your side too."

"You're not Mr. Whyte?" Her voice warbled in the wind. Thunder rumbled in the distance.

"No. I don't know who that is," said Ryan. "Could we open the door now?"

Silence.

I nodded at Ryan, and he tried the door again.

It creaked open, and he stepped back into the shadows as I took over.

52

When the door stretched all the way open, I caught sight of her painfully young, pale face a foot above mine. Mascara dripped down her round cheeks. Her hair was slicked against her head.

"Please come with me," I said. "We'll get you help."

She shook her head, flinging rain into the night.

"Okay. Just come out of the rain."

She held up her index finger and crooked it toward me. "Could you ... help me?"

"Yes, I want to help you. Come in."

"No." She made the beckoning gesture again. The full moon hung over her shoulder.

I frowned. "You want me to come out?"

"I ... " Her voice dipped back into silence. At last, she whispered, barely audible, "Help me."

I glanced at Ryan. He shook his head.

"It's not a good idea to go out on the roof. Please." I reached my left hand toward her, nearly touching her skinny, white arm now clad in a soaked black T-shirt.

"Please! I'm scared."

"No, Hope." Ryan took my other hand firmly.

I started at his touch. It made my skin sing and my heart flutter, even though he squeezed my fingers only to anchor me.

Oh, I was screwed. I closed my eyes, opened them, and concentrated on Cloud. "I can't come out. You have to come in."

Cloud slowly laced her fingers in mine.

"Great!" I held her tight and started to walk backward, drawing her in. Ryan backed up with me.

"Help!" she called.

I started to shake my hand free from Ryan so I could give her both hands.

Then she hauled on my left hand.

I screamed as I pitched toward the opening.

53

Cloud snarled back at me, still dragging me toward her.

This girl wanted to toss me face-first from the second floor. I howled into the night air as I launched my weight back toward Ryan, trying to rip away from her.

She maintained a death grip on my left hand.

My shoulder popped but didn't dislocate. Wind swept the rain into my face in the split second before I yanked my left hand so hard that my neck twinged.

She clung on.

Ryan cinched his arms around my waist and heaved me back. I stiffened in pain, but with another wrench from both of us, my left hand slipped out of her wet one.

Free. Ryan backed us away from the opening, beyond her reach. I pressed against him and shivered. I didn't dare move my neck, which didn't hurt as long as I kept it rigidly upright. My teeth began to rattle.

She tried to *kill* me.

"Call 911," I whispered, my throat already raw. They could take her off the roof. Not me. My hands shook too much, or I'd call them myself.

"No. Hope. Please!" Cloud's cry reached our ears.

"No," I said. Ryan's arms encircled my waist, and I closed my eyes, savouring the feel of his body even as I trembled.

"You tried to kill Hope," Ryan snapped. He kept his left arm around me as he grabbed his phone with his right.

How could I have been so dumb as to reach for a killer? Just because she was small and seemed helpless? If she'd been stronger—if I'd weighed less—if Ryan hadn't tethered me—

"I didn't mean to. I'm sorry!" She crouched in the doorway, silhouetted by moonlight. "Please help me."

"Yes. Police, please," Ryan told his phone as we backed down the stairs, his other arm still laced around me.

"How could you not *mean* to pull me off?" I muttered at her. I could still feel the raised imprint of her fingers on mine.

She shouted back, "He said to scare you."

"Who?"

"Mr. Whyte."

Mr. Whyte. She'd confirmed my stalker's name. I sagged in response.

Ryan kissed my neck, almost reflexively. I gasped as a different kind of arrow shot through my core. My toes curled in my shoes. We both froze.

Cloud broke into our thoughts. "I wanted to scare you. I wasn't going to kill you. Please!"

"I believe you," said a female voice beneath us, on the stairs. "I'm here."

We all jerked to attention. Ryan and I hastily danced up the stairwell.

The moon's glow revealed Jennifer's sober face. I caught my breath. The floor vibrated as she stepped beside us, her eyes fixed on Cloud's figure in the doorway. "It's okay, Cloud."

Easy for Jennifer to say. She hadn't been the one dangling out the rooftop door. I bit my lip and searched for empathy. Not gonna lie, it was easier since Ryan had accidentally kissed me.

Jennifer moved past Ryan and me without acknowledgement. "I'll take it from here."

"No! She'll pull you out. She grabbed me." I swiped for Jennifer's hand.

She evaded me. Ryan murmured to the 911 operator while turning his head to watch Jennifer, gauging if he could hold her.

"I can help you, Cloud." Jennifer stood in front of the door, within arm's reach of the teenager. The girl's hands clutched the door frame on both sides, but any second, she could fall forward and seize Jennifer.

Ryan and I stilled once more.

I didn't want to get any closer to that goddamn roof door. But I might have to do it to save Jennifer.

"I'll do it," Ryan muttered.

"No." He was bigger and stronger, but I couldn't handle him smashing his head or breaking his body. *Take me instead.*

Jennifer extended her right hand to Cloud. "You want to get out of here, right? I know the way out."

"I'm scared," said Cloud, retreating onto the roof ledge and out of sight.

I breathed a little easier. Not that I wanted Cloud to fall, but my greater fear was one of us falling with her.

"We're all scared," Jennifer said calmly. Rain dripped through the open door, hitting her in the face, but she didn't recoil. She waited quietly, her face turned up to the moonlight so that Cloud could see her expression.

"I should jump," said Cloud. "I deserve to die."

I exhaled and shook my head. She'd been forced into underage prostitution. If I were alone and starving and facing a cattle prod, I'd kill that guy too.

Thunder boomed. Cloud's silhouette flinched. She huddled closer to the roof.

"No one deserves to die," said Jennifer. "Least of all you. Let me get you some dry clothes and some people who can help." She held both palms up now.

"What if I jump instead?" Cloud called. "No one would care."

"I'd care," said Jennifer. Ryan nodded, although he was also talking to the 911 operator and still hugging me from behind. I couldn't resist leaning against him infinitesimally.

Cloud snorted. "That's *bullshit*. No one would miss me."

"I'd miss you," said Jennifer.

"You don't even know me!"

"I know that you're scared and need a second chance. We all need someone. I can be that someone for you."

"No, you'll throw me to the cops. They'll put me away forever for what I did to that guy."

I closed my eyes at Cloud's admission of guilt.

"I'm not sending you to the police," said Jennifer. "I tried it with two other people before you, but it didn't work out. So instead, I'll get you to a safe place where you're warm and clean and dry and can have something to eat before you sleep."

"Hamoudi's shawarma?" asked Cloud.

Jennifer laughed. "I'll do my best. Then you can make your own decisions if you want to talk to the police."

"No! I'm never talking to them!"

"That's fine. It's up to you. My job is to get you to a safe space. That's all."

No one spoke for a full minute. There was even a moment of silence from the bar below after the DJ finished playing "Mony, Mony."

"Ryan, can you hear me?" a tinny voice asked through the phone speaker beside me. "Are you still there?"

I cursed to myself. The 911 operator was perfectly audible to me, and probably to Cloud, despite the rain and wind.

"That guy is bringing in the cops!" Cloud shouted. She knew that 911 automatically triggered the police, although I've heard that their immediate location ability isn't as fine-tuned as TV would have you believe.

Jennifer didn't turn around. "Ryan, please hang up."

"They'll send someone anyway," he said.

"Hang up, please. We don't need more cops here."

I twisted to face him. My neck pinged again, but not as badly as before. I blinked back the pain while Ryan silently asked my opinion with his eyes.

Cloud could try to pull Jennifer out. But my money was on Jennifer. Her calm steadfastness seemed to be getting through.

I nodded at Ryan.

He shook his head. But in the end, he hit the red button and cut the call.

"We don't have much time," Jennifer told Cloud. "An officer is on the way. But I can bring you to a safe place. Will you come with me?"

A crackle of lightning behind her made me flinch.

Wind ushered raindrops toward me and Ryan.

Cloud's head appeared in the doorway. She hesitated. "I never want to see Mr. Whyte again."

"I'll do my very best," said Jennifer.

Cloud's pale hands grasped the doorframe, and she leapt inside.

54

Cloud slid on the wet wood before Jennifer steadied her with a hand on her arm, which she removed as soon as Cloud was upright. "Ryan and Hope. Could you please send away the police officer? Ryan, it was your phone. You'll have to make up a story."

"How do I know you'll be safe?" Ryan asked Jennifer, glancing at Cloud. Jennifer might trust Cloud, but we didn't.

Cloud snorted. She was shorter and thinner than I was. "Yeah, that's right. I'm a big threat." Rain fell from her hands, spattering the floorboards.

"I'll text you," said Jennifer, pointing Cloud down the stairs.

We followed them, Ryan first. I knew that he wanted to keep Cloud away from me as he argued, "But if I've already sent the cops away—"

"Keep them on site, then. Tell them I have new information for them about the skeleton in the chimney." Jennifer lowered the trap door.

My mouth fell open at that. It was the last thing I'd expected. "Do you?"

"In a sense. It's more like old information. I'll speak to the police in 45 minutes or less." She steered Cloud toward the rope ladder.

Cloud waved at me. "No hard feelings."

I shook my head instead of answering.

"We could follow you," said Ryan.

"No!" Jennifer's voice cracked through the air like a whip. "I need you to get rid of the cops. Can you go do that, or do I have to call someone else to run interference?"

"We'll do our best," I said finally.

"Do that, and you'll be rewarded." Then she headed down the rope ladder, murmuring to Cloud.

Everything bothered me. Was Jennifer truly taking Cloud to a safe place? My instincts said yes, but I couldn't be sure. Not to mention that Cloud was a live wire

Ryan cursed under his breath.

Should Cloud be allowed to escape from the police?

Cloud had killed a torturer who no doubt wanted to hurt, scar, rape, and possibly kill her. I wouldn't mourn him.

The system is nowhere close to perfect. Marginalized people languish behind bars while rich white collar criminals run free. I would let her go.

But for Ryan, my Christian law-abiding love, this was a whole other level of wrong.

I craned my sore neck around, trying to catch his eye. "I know this must be trippy for you. First Rogue Con, then—"

"Then I don't know what to think," he said finally, letting go of my waist.

My temperature dropped 10 degrees, and I hugged myself as I forced myself to take a step away from him.

"You have a stalker," Ryan said.

"Yes. Since at least January. Apparently by Mr. Whyte."

"What the actual f—" He bit down on the last word.

I smiled anyway. "Yeah."

"And he's going to show his face at some point?"

"I assume so. This weekend was a lot of work for him. He probably wants to take credit for it, although he *could* taunt me indefinitely instead." Gah.

I exhaled. At least then I'd found the new direction for the rest of my life. I'd become a family/emergency doctor and I'd go after this sicko. With or without a man at my side.

Ryan cleared his throat. "I didn't know you were in danger since January."

We stared at each other. I took in his taut face and the darkness in his eyes and said, "I didn't know it either when we broke up. It's not your fault. And I don't want to overcall it, since the stalker hasn't physically hurt me yet."

Ryan threw up his hands. "There's one man dead, and Cloud tried to toss you off the roof."

There was that.

"He's escalating. He uses other people like props, including that—Tucker," Ryan said, choosing his words carefully. "He's building up to a grand finale, which is probably the destruction of you."

Objectively, that made sense. "Yep. Which is why I should probably get you out of here. He's manipulating you too."

"We came here after Marina got the blueprints—"

I held up my palms. "Why did she even buy into the Rumrunner's Rest in the first place?"

He had to think about it. "She was doing research. She'd put the word out at the college that this was her passion project. One of the students sent her a book with a copy of the first blueprints."

"Who was the student?"

"I can find out. No, wait. She mentioned him today. Wy Leighton."

My eyes practically popped as I jerked around to face him, heat surging through my body. I could hardly speak. "Wy Leighton. Mr. Whyte. Jazz said I was 'lightly amusing.' And ... " My blood iced over. "My brother Kevin is coming here for a Mr. *Ng*. The whole time, that bastard's been spelling it out. Wy Leighton. Whyte 'lightly' Ng."

Ryan's brow drew together, so I spat the words out for him. *"White Lightning."*

55

"White Lightning," Ryan repeated. "The drink they serve here?"

I was already calling Kevin. "Yes. And the bootlegger rumrunner pilot who disappeared in 1928." My phone wouldn't even connect to his new number. It paused without ringing, maybe because of the pouring rain outside. "And the name of the man who may or may not be related to Tucker." Finally, it started to ring. "All the same person. White Lightning. Fuck!"

The ringing stuttered, paused, and barely managed to ring again.

"Fuck!" I called my dad. Same thing.

My mother. Same.

I texted all of them. *Are you alive?*

No answer.

"The stalker has my family! My God!"

I can handle me being in danger. But my hard-working father? My well-meaning mother? And my precocious little brother, one of my favourite people in the entire world?

My fear revved into overdrive. *Take me. Take me, you sick bastard. Don't take it out on teenaged girls and my nine-year-old brother. I'm right here.*

"Think, Hope, think!" I cried aloud, trying Kevin's number again.

"Is Kevin in Ottawa?" Ryan asked.

I wish. Eight hours away. "No. They're driving here." I paged through the messages from Kevin's new phone earlier this evening.

Mr. Ng. He's taking all of us out in his Zénobe for an epic steak dinner!

"He's taking them in his electric car. A Zénobe."

Ryan gave a low whistle. "There can't be too many of those around."

I remembered the parking lot earlier this evening, that space near the front reserved for electric cars. "I'll stake out his car."

"I'll go with you."

"Call the police. Please." I started down the rope ladder, jumping off halfway down. Ryan landed beside me and bundled up the ladder.

"He won't play if you're there," I told him. "You can go check on Marina."

"No. I'll call 911 and stand by you. We need to outsmart him. I texted Marina. She might have some ideas."

That irritated me, despite the fact that I could use every hand on deck. I texted Tucker, who replied, *Wut.*

Me: *Parking lot.*

The stalker had bought Kevin a phone. Hell, he'd bought all of them new phones. He must be spying on them with some malware, chortling every time I reached out to them.

Time to provoke him by calling him out.

I messaged all three immediate members of my family.

Whyte Leighton Ng. Your problem is with me. Leave my father, mother, and brother out of this.

Parking lot. Now.

56

As I flew down the stairs to the ground floor, Ryan kept pace behind me. He's a runner. He could probably sprint three flights before me.

"I know you hate me," I threw over my shoulder.

"I don't hate you." He paused before racing down the last few steps. "I miss you," he said finally.

"I miss you too." I could see the side door, but I hung back. "I want you to be happy, though. You deserve it."

He smiled at me. "Yeah."

We both laughed.

"You'll always be my ... " I didn't know what to say. *My first love. The one I want. The one I trust. My baby. My maybe.* I shook my head. "I know that I should let you go. It's smart that you blocked me. I couldn't ... "

"Yeah. That was tough."

But he didn't say he'd unblock me. He didn't promise to take me back. He didn't tell me he still loved me.

My tears fell (again! Still! Sorry!) and he stretched his hand toward me, momentarily reminding me of Jennifer and Cloud, before his arm dropped back to his side. "Take care of yourself, Hope."

Miraculously, no police officer guarded the door. Ryan held it open for me.

This might be the last time I ever saw him. At least alone. Our individual futures stretched out before us. It was my moment to let him go gracefully.

I took a deep breath and sabotaged that chance. "I love you," I said right before I sailed through the door.

Maybe he heard me, maybe he didn't.

Either way, he didn't answer.

And I had my family to save.

57

Rain slapped me in the face.

I smeared my hand over my eyes, clearing my vision. In the distance, thunder grumbled.

My phone rang and rang, calling for Kevin, but no one answered.

Wait. I had another way to track my nearest and dearest. I switched over to the Finding Friends app and sighed in relief when my brother's dot glowed in real time on my phone's map.

I knew Kevin himself might not be in the parking lot. The app only tracked his phone. The stalker might have taken his phone, luring me toward him.

Tori was in the hospital, Griffin beside her. Tucker had run off to investigate Josie. I'd probably scared off Ryan forever.

It was just me in the darkness, trying to find my brother before it was too late.

Exactly as Mr. Ng had planned.

Lightning struck in the distance, followed by a boom of thunder. I flinched, but the Rumrunner's tall roof should attract any strikes. Right?

I hurried toward Kevin's map dot, located at the edge of the parking lot. It directed me to a neon yellow car under the streetlamp.

Nestled in the electric vehicle parking space, its license plate read WTLNG.

My heart dropped, but I gritted my teeth. Bingo. I circled the car, trying to peer inside its tinted windows. I could use that bolt of lightning to help illuminate things right now.

My phone crackled on speaker phone, and I held it to my ear, only to hear, "Hi, it's Kevin. Leave a message!"

"Kevin, come out," I called, both to his voice mail and to the car in front of me. "It's Hope. I'm here. Come out now."

I heard the electric whir as the rear window on the driver's side descended. I hastened over to that dark space, not daring to get too close. "Kevin? Get out!"

My brother's head and left hand popped out the window. A white flower dropped out of his fingers before his little voice said, "Hope?"

58

Kevin had grown his hair into a bowl cut, which was truly unfortunate, and he'd gotten a bit chubbier than I'd realized in our video calls. That didn't matter. He was here. He was alive.

I raced toward him and grabbed the door handle. The Zénobe is fancy, but it still has a door handle, although it was vertical instead of horizontal for some stupid reason.

I jerked on it. "Open up, Kevin." The door handle clicked uselessly.

A man chuckled from the driver's seat as the rain drove down on me.

Not today, Satan. "Let's go, Kev." I managed to sound calm. Mostly.

"Hope, I missed you!" he said back. I always worry that he'll grow up too much in between me seeing him, but he was still a little kid.

"I missed you too," I said, yanking on the driver's door handle. Also locked. "Come here."

"I can't. Mr. Ng is taking us out for a steak dinner, remember?"

"No. Kevin, get out now!"

"No, Hope, you get in." He stuck his head out further. I wanted to cry at the straight cut of his bangs and his soft, vulnerable nose and ears as he said, "I'll go in the middle, and we'll pick up Mom and Dad."

"Kevin. CELERY." I willed him to make the connection. "You're in a CELERY CAR." *You're in a stalker car. Get out, get out.*

His eyes widened. He remembered. Stalker. He instinctively protested, "No, Mr. Ng!"

"Celery," I repeated. "Open the door." I grabbed the handle again, planting my right foot against the fancy yellow car finish, praying to the rain gods for strength, but the door didn't budge.

"Mr. Ng? Wynn?" Kevin's voice quavered, as he worked the door handle from the inside. "Can you let me out?"

The driver's window lowered. Four white flowers dropped into the rain.

I stopped breathing for a second. I did not want to see the stalker's face. Didn't want to breathe the same air as him.

I jerked my head at Kevin, urging him to climb out the window.

His seat belt clicked as he released it.

Movement in my left peripheral vision caught my eye. The driver extended his arm past the window frame into the air, displaying a silver crossbow.

I caught my breath. I knew that crossbow.

Mr. Ng was either the Hush guy who wore a white mask, or he'd taken that guy's crossbow.

Either way, not a good sign. I twisted my head away from the arm and the crossbow, determined not to react. If he was displaying the crossbow, he wasn't shooting it.

But I had to get my brother out of the fucking car pronto.

I pressed the emergency buttons on my phone. "I'm calling the police for *child kidnapping.*"

Kevin tried to pitch himself through the window, which was perfect because he was small and the window was the only opening.

"That's it! Come on!" I shoved the phone in my pocket, ignoring its squawk. They'd send someone now that I'd called. Hell, there should be police on site. Any second now—

Kevin thrust his head and his neck out of the window, and I reached to haul him all the way out.

Mr. Ng rolled the window up on Kevin's neck.

59

Kevin screamed until his cry got choked off.
 Oh, my God. I flashed back to our last and most terrible ER case where a toddler had died from a power window. Kevin was nine, but—

I jammed down on the window edge as hard as I could and howled loud enough that the entire Rumrunner's Rest should hear me.

Then I reached into my jeans pocket and yanked out my car keys.

"Kevin, close your eyes!" I shouted. I barely had time to seal my own before I smashed the window.

Not with my hands. With the CarResCue. I pressed its black end against the window, like their video had instructed me, and the entire window pane shattered.

Kevin hollered as he hit the window frame with a crunch of broken glass, but I was already yanking him out by his shoulders.

Cubes of safety glass rained on my feet and on my jean-clad legs. I didn't care. He was breathing. He was moving. He was alive. *My brother. Was. Alive. And. Free.*

I ignored the wrench in my back and shoulder as Kevin's feet hit the ground. He toppled forward, catching himself on his hands.

I threw myself between Kevin and the car and snarled, "Run!"

The car sprang to life. Its front lights rotated upward and illuminated the night as it reversed and then pointed its nose toward me.

I braced myself for the car to run me over. And then run Kevin over.

I stood rooted anyway.

If my body delayed the stalker hitting Kevin by one millisecond, or one metre per second, I'd take it.

The car blinded me. All I could see were its headlights and the faint glow of the stalker's mask behind the dark windshield. My tears mixed with the rain but I stood, defiant.

"Go, Kevin," I yelled, partly a prayer, partly a command.

Then the stalker opened his door and stepped out with his crossbow, his car still running.

Since he wasn't immediately running us over or shooting us, I turned and pelted after Kevin as rain stung my dazzled eyes.

Run like your life depends on it. Because it does.

Should we zigzag to throw off his aim? When I tried, my shoes skidded on the wet asphalt. I fell.

Pavement scraped my palms and knees. My neck spronged again, and my back and right shoulder joined the chorus, but in a distant way, like my body belonged to someone else. Adrenaline is almost as good as ketamine.

Kevin spun back to help me up.

"RUN!" I screamed, but he raised his face to the sky, his body completely still as he gawked behind me.

I seized his arm, trying to hurry him along like a four-legged race when two of the legs are locked in place.

"Please, Kevin!" I begged as I tried to tow him. "Come on, Kevin! This way."

His arm flapped with me, but he couldn't seem to move.

I tried to pick Kevin up, no, ouch, not lifting him around the waist, that wouldn't work.

I stooped and tried to bend him over my right shoulder. That was what fire fighters did, right?

"Bend! C'mon! Celery, remember?"

His knees relaxed a touch. I straightened my own legs, hefting Kevin up, and I could hear him saying, "Hope, no, Hope," but I ignored him and took a step. Then another.

Slower than a fire fighter. Slower than an obese raccoon. The stalker would catch us any second.

Police, please. But no sirens sliced through the night air. My phone must've died before they located us.

No 911 would save us. The Rogues, including Tucker, remained safely shut inside, none of them able to hear us above the thunder. Ryan gunned toward us, speeding through the rain, but still impossibly far away.

Rain slewed against my face. I couldn't tell if I was crying anymore. I screamed again, but the wind whipped the sound away.

The air sizzled. My hair seemed to lift. I couldn't speak, almost like electrons danced in my throat.

And lightning struck.

60

The light in my peripheral vision temporarily blinded me. I couldn't hear, smell, or feel anything else for that split second. Only light.

Thunder smashed the ground, making the earth and my chest, my lungs, my legs vibrate with its force before I crashed.

I swallowed to release the pressure in my ears as I blinked away the darkness. I heard sobbing. It took me a second to realize that it was me.

I was lying on the ground with my brother on top of me.

"Kevin," I huffed. "You okay?"

I couldn't rise with him pinning me down, so I cautiously eased my way out from under him.

He was breathing, but his mouth was open as he pointed back toward the stalker.

"Forget him!" I shouted, as Ryan sprinted at us, Tucker at his heels.

Ryan helped Kevin to his feet and held out a hand for me.

Even with his help, I stumbled on my way up, especially when Tucker launched himself at me and tossed his arms around my neck. "Hope. Oh my God, Hope."

I released Ryan's hand with an apologetic smile. The corner of his mouth twisted in understanding before Kevin cannonballed at me. "Hope!"

"Kevin." I squeezed him, inhaling his wet hair and his little boy smell. I didn't realize that I was hurting him until he wriggled in protest.

Blue Guy and G String held open the door of the Rumrunner's Rest for us.

I yelled, "You have to get the driver. He's in the yellow Zénobe in the parking lot—or he was—he had Kevin, he kidnapped him, he could have killed him—"

"He was struck by lightning!" G String shouted back before covering her mouth. "We need a doctor!"

I am a doctor, and no way in hell.

Tucker wrapped his arm around my side. I leaned against him, rubbing my cheek against his rough one, before I filled my arms with Kevin and said, "Thanks, Ryan."

Ryan offered me a half-smile and nod before he pulled out his phone, no doubt texting Marina.

"No one should go out in that rain," said Blue Guy.

"He might die," G String said, her eyes wide, no playfulness now.

He might, I agreed silently in my head, before I said aloud, "Call 911."

Someone did. I could hear a guy telling them about the man who was struck by lightning.

As two new police cruisers screeched into the parking lot, G String said, "He laughed as he held his crossbow above his head with both hands. I swear he was going to shoot you!"

"It was already cocked with a bolt in," Blue Guy agreed.

"Except this little boy came out of nowhere," said G String.

A little boy. I raised my eyebrows at Kevin.

"Not him," said G String. "A smaller boy."

"I couldn't tell what it was," said Joan.

"Too hazy," Kathy agreed.

A bespectacled woman with red and black hair stepped in. "No, it was a tiny boy who looked like—you know those Hallowe'en decorations made out of chicken wire?"

"Yeah, like a greyish white outline with a lot of black holes," said a tall, bald man with a goatee.

"Those were black marks on his face and hands." said Blue Guy.

I thought of Tori in her not-blackface.

G String took back the story. "The little boy just sort of *appeared*. His feet didn't even touch the ground. I was going to point that out, but then he raised his hands to the sky. The boy brought his arms down at the *exact same time* as lightning struck your man's crossbow. Did you see him?"

Kevin nodded up at me. He'd seen it, too. That was what had paralyzed him.

"Someone needs to go after that little boy. I couldn't see him after the lightning faded away," G String said.

"I'll do it," Blue Guy offered, but before a search party could form, two police officers firmly ordered everyone to stay inside.

No one would ever find that little boy. With any luck, he'd gone to a far, far better place after helping us.

Thank you, I said in my heart, patting Kevin's wet hair. *Thank you for saving our lives. Rest in peace, Edwin.*

61

"Can I go see Mom and Dad?" Kevin asked after the cops had finished questioning the four of us.

Ryan nodded goodbye to me. I couldn't resist one last look at him before the officer, S. Mahoney, escorted Tucker, Kevin and me to the Rumrunner's Rest restaurant on the opposite side of the ground floor, where my parents enjoyed their main course with a bottle of red wine.

"Why did you leave your son alone in a car with a stranger?" asked S. Mahoney after introducing herself and explaining our circumstances.

My father wiped his mouth with a napkin, surprised. "Wynn wasn't a stranger. He was a family friend."

"How long had you known him?"

Dad had to think. "Since the Christmas holidays?"

My mother cut in. "The first steak was when Hope was in Egypt. It was like butter! I told him we'd like to bring Grandma next time. He said sure!"

"You should never leave your children unsupervised with an unknown adult," said S. Mahoney. "You have to protect them from pedophiles. Your daughter says he was stalking her and was concerned that he preyed on your son."

I squeezed Kevin's hand. He pulled away from me and mouthed "I'm fine," before he plopped in a chair. He looked for a menu, but settled for picking pieces out of our mom's baked potato.

The officer told us to come to the station to give statements as soon as we finished here. My head throbbed. I was getting good at police statements. But in the meantime, I could smell steak. I sighed and sank into the chair Tucker pulled out for me.

"You had a stalker?" Mom cut off a piece of carrot and offered it to me.

I chewed it gratefully. I couldn't remember the last time I'd eaten, and a buttered carrot tasted like heaven. Tucker poured us a glass of water.

"What do you mean by a stalker?" asked Mom.

Tucker smiled at her. "It's someone who's obsessed with you and follows you everywhere, in person, online, or both."

Mom frowned while allocating us pieces of her steak on her bread plate. "Why did he want you so much?"

"I don't know." My wet clothes clung to my arms and hips. With any luck, my hair wouldn't drip on the table, but I felt bone weary.

"Rich man. He could have had anyone. He was married!"

"Great." I shook water out of my ears.

"Why would he want you?"

I didn't feel up to explaining to my mother that stalkers are not logical. Marriage doesn't stop an obsession. Wealth probably makes it worse. They're so used to buying everything they want, why not another human being?

I gazed around the wood-panelled room. The entire romanticized bootlegging craze was an industry based on greed. People didn't care what they did, as long as they got paid. Money flowed in like water and immediately evaporated, spent on a pretty girl, nice duds, another airplane, or bribes.

"Wynn could have had anyone at the Mackenzie Corporation. I wondered why he was calling our house," Mom added.

"What?" Mackenzie's fire-X logo flashed into my mind. The stalker had even sponsored the chimney opening.

Kevin had texted me, *He's* 🔥*!*

My brother had given me more clues than I'd realized.

"Oh, you know. Wynn would call and ask for you, I'd say you weren't home, and he'd ask about my sewing. He might joke about work with your father or ask about Kevin's violin. He seemed like such a gentlemen. And then he paid for us to go to that steakhouse. He didn't even come, but sent us the gift certificates. Everything was paid for."

"Even dessert," Kevin said, more quietly.

WTLNG, as I decided to call the stalker, had infiltrated my family so thoroughly that my own mother was convinced he was a good guy. No matter that he'd throttled Kevin with his car window, my mother still waxed nostalgic about free food.

"He promised to take us out again. And he paid for our hotel room this weekend. Oh! I wonder if he'll still pay now that it's all—" She waved her hand.

I sighed. "I'll pay for it, Mom. I can take it out of my line of credit."

"Don't be silly! We can afford it." She shook her head wistfully.

It's hard for me and Tucker as perpetually indebted students. But it must be hard for our parents, too. Mine have scrimped to help hammer down my debt. It hadn't occurred to me that they, too, would be swayed by a fancy car and a juicy steak.

Now I knew. Almost too late.

But I could protect my family going forward.

My father rose from his chair to gave me a rough hug. He smelled like soap.

"I'm okay, Dad," I told his shoulder, my voice rough.

Jennifer appeared behind us with a teapot and cups on a tray, which she set on the table. "I'm so sorry," she said, gesturing for me and my dad to sit. "I can only stay a minute, but I want to assure you, I had no idea what Mr. Wyatt Lyte had planned. I never would have accepted money from him on behalf of the Mackenzie Corporation."

I stirred a bunch of sugar into my tea, which I don't usually drink, but I needed the warmth and calories. As I sipped it, I closed my eyes. "Mr. Wyatt Lyte."

"Yes, I apologize profoundly. I've worked with STIP for years, but I might have undone it all tonight with Mr. Lyte."

I was too tired to argue that point. "He called himself Wynn Ng with my parents. Was he Asian?"

Kevin laughed, our parents shook their heads, and Jennifer shifted her weight to her right leg. "Mr. Lyte appeared Caucasian."

I silently pointed at the chair at a neighbouring table, asking her to sit. She pulled the chair over, but sat a foot away from our crowded table.

I tapped my chin. "I think the stalker figured out who was in the chimney. Then he sent all of us on a wild goose chase. He got Marina and Ryan interested. He funded the chimney opening. Right after donating to STIP, he thought it was funny to send—" I didn't say Cloud's name, but Jennifer knew who I meant. "—someone underage to test me before he trapped Kevin." I turned to my brother. "Did he hurt you?"

... young, beautiful, strong, covered with white blossoms ...

My brother looked up, still chewing on our dad's fries. "What? No. He's really good at TF2. I thought he was a bot at first. He dominated the leader board. But we teamed up and started winning."

"TF2," I repeated.

"Team Fortress 2."

"A video game," Tucker explained, after I'd already figured that out.

"We shut down all of my accounts," I said, "but we left Kevin's. How did he contact you?"

Kevin pushed my mom's plate away. "Discord, I think."

"Was that how he normally talked to you?"

"Um, sometimes we used WhatsApp or Snapchat or whatever."

My father frowned. "I didn't know that."

Kevin rubbed his face. "He seemed like a good guy. He came to our school to talk about the Mackenzie Corporation. He gave us his email so we could contact him. Mom and Dad met him. They thought he was okay. And he gave us free stuff."

Yeah. My family was dazzled by the free stuff, and by the attention from a rich, powerful white man.

Kevin grabbed my hand. His skin was even colder than mine. "Mr. Ng said we should come down for this trip. He told Dad it wasn't good to work all the time. You know Mom likes to get away. He said there were good drinks here or something? The Bearcat?"

I hid my grimace. It felt like a lifetime ago that I'd choked down half a Bearcat. "Did he touch you?"

"No!"

"Not even when he was alone in the car with you?"

"No." He paused. "Well, he always ruffled my hair. He got me this haircut, even though it's lame. And helped me with the fancy seat belt in the Zénobe the first time. He kind of—"

"Kind of what?" Dad snapped. My mother watched, eyes wide.

Kevin squeezed my hand instead of answering at first. "Held on for a minute with his hands on my stomach. But he didn't touch me down there."

Yet.

I grabbed Kevin, pressing my face against his hair.

I'd assumed the stalker wanted me. But maybe what he really wanted was my brother.

Pedophiles often picked victims who wouldn't speak up, wouldn't be believed, or wouldn't be missed. Poor kids, runaways, kids who'd already been abused.

WTLNG had chosen the opposite: my brother, a beloved boy with a detective sister and careless parents. Mr. Ng had set the highest challenge for himself to feast on my brother's innocence.

Even his name was a clue. Not only a truncated version of White Lightning, but he'd literally called himself Wynn Ng. Winning.

"Aw, Hope!" Kevin wriggled.

I kissed his ear.

"Gross!"

I turned to our mom. "I think he did it because ... he wanted to beat me and prove he could still get what he wanted."

WTLNG must've grown tired of shoving everyone else off the corporate ladder. Then I popped up on his radar as a kind of idiot savant sleuth with a delicious young brother. WTLNG groomed Kevin and my parents for months. He literally could have kidnapped, raped, and killed Kevin any time.

Instead, WTLNG set up this weekend as an elaborate game, toying with me and my nearest and dearest. He invited Tucker and Tori, plus Ryan to haunt me. He made sure Marina and Ryan found the bones. He funded the skeleton's unveiling. He set up a microphone in our room and Jazz's multimedia show in her own trailer.

Cloud was a clue that children were part of his game, to remind me of the one child I loved most. I was supposed to fight for Kevin the second before WTLNG abused and/or killed him in front of my eyes.

Why such an intricate plan? I couldn't explain it, except I know that some people would yank the wings off a fly for fun. Boom, done. Yet others would relish prolonging the game, first by outwitting a supposed genius in order to obtain the fly and then by torturing the fly for hours in front of her.

He almost got away with it. The one thing he hadn't factored in was Tori's inexplicable connection to Edwin's ghost.

Edwin knew how it felt to be bought and sold like a piece of licorice. He knew men who spent their days overworking and exploiting children. Something about WTLNG had called Edwin here from beyond the grave, across the ocean, and through the centuries.

Now WTLNG was at least in hospital and, with any luck, motherfucking dead.

"Thank you, Edwin," I whispered aloud, before letting Kevin go. He pounced on his water glass. *Edwin, thank you for shattering him with a bolt of lightning in a storm.*

"You're very welcome, my dear," said a slim, curvy, masked Black woman who pressed a note beside Dad's plate before continuing on by.

I gasped. Her voice. That compelling, siren-like voice of the woman in the trailer.

I leapt to my feet, snatching the note. "Jazz. Wait."

"Hope, before I go, I want you to have something," said Jennifer, rising to her feet.

I shook my head and jumped from the table, knocking back my chair. Tucker caught it while Mom sighed and Kevin said, "Hope?"

Jennifer blocked my way, holding out a leather-bound book.

I sidestepped her, but Jazz's bob disappeared out the restaurant door. I dashed after her as Rogues flowed in my path, including a Miss Hannigan literally clutching her pearls.

"Jazz! Wait! Excuse me!"

Blocked by the avalanche of humanity in the doorway, I hustled toward the relatively empty wall, tripped on a bench leg, and caught myself against the wall with both hands.

Ow, protested my neck, palms, and back. When I pushed myself up, I scooped up Jazz's crumpled note. Ignoring the sting in my wrists, I read the printed serif font:

Thanks for freeing us from Frederick Grant

Frederick Grant.

Jazz had handed me one final gift, the stalker's true name. I'd pass that on to the police in my interview. I needed to tell them—

A memory prodded me, but before I could grasp it, a woman's voice broke into my thoughts. A friendly voice, a familiar voice, not a mind-bending voice like Jazz's.

"Are you all right?" Jennifer's forehead creased with concern.

"Fine." I tried to hold the paper with only my fingertips, even though I doubted Jazz had left any fingerprints behind.

"You ran away. Do you really not want this?" She held out her book again.

"What is it?" Now that I looked closer, I noticed its brown leather cover, worn at the edges.

Jennifer laughed. "It's a diary. My parents found it when they bought the Rumrunner's Rest."

My brain stalled. Too much information. "Your parents own the Rumrunner's Rest?"

"You thought I did? I don't have the capital to own a place like this."

I'd never thought about Jennifer much at all, so I parried, "I heard Marina Ma was a part owner." No wonder they let Ryan cut the power.

"Yes, she owns 20 percent now. We need money for renovations." She sighed. "Let's not talk about that now. Do you want the diary?"

"Hell, yeah." I grinned and accepted it with my free hand.

62

The next morning, I brought fruit and orchids for Tori, who sat in her all-white hospital bed on a cardiac monitor, waiting for the team to round on her.

She picked up an orange and smiled at the white and purple orchids. "Thank you. Help yourselves."

Griffin grabbed a banana, avoiding our eyes. "Thanks."

"You okay?" I asked her.

She lifted one eyebrow. "Tucker told me you went through the wringer again, thanks to someone named Frederick Grant."

I nodded reluctantly. "It's not as bad as what happened to you."

Griffin met my gaze. "I looked him up while Tori was sleeping. 'Rick Grant' is a big fish at the Mackenzie Corporation."

"The Chief Business Officer," said Tucker.

"Chief Pedophile," I said, before I snapped my mouth shut.

"Okay." Tori raised her eyebrows, but I shook my head. Chief Pedophile had been airlifted to the burn unit in Toronto. Last I heard, he was in critical but stable condition. As long as he was alive, and his minions and electronic spies might linger, I didn't feel comfortable saying much in public.

"We'll talk about something else." Tori gazed at the sink on the wall across from her. "The bones in the fireplace still bother me."

"Me too," I said. "I think it's White Lightning, who was one of three brothers, but which one? How old were the brothers when White Lightning disappeared?"

Tori's eyes lit up, and my heart sang to see her intelligence back full-force. "I know this. Frederick was 31, Louis was 29, and William was 27."

Tucker, Tori and I were 27 now, which was sort of eerie. And what about the fact that one of the brothers had the same name as my stalker?

Could be coincidence. I moved on. "So they were all old enough to go white during Prohibition. Any of them could have been White Lightning. Right?"

Tucker nodded. "If we're related, Tuckers usually go white by 25, 30 at the outside."

"And they were all old enough to fight in World War I," said Griffin. "The youngest would have been underage, but that never stopped them."

Tori shook her head. "That's exactly the problem. Which one of them was White Lightning?"

"Could it even be some strange thing where they took turns being White Lightning?" I wondered aloud.

Tori pressed her lips together. "Maybe. But only one of them would have disappeared. They were from the area. People here would know them individually. In Chicago and Detroit, they only saw the hair, but here, they'd be Frederick, Louis, and William."

Tucker unfolded the newspaper cutting that had been hidden in the hole of our room. "I think we're missing something here. WTLNG was playing us. We were smart enough to find his hidden microphone, so he handed us a clue. There has to be more than a description of how White Lightning made his fortune."

Tori and Griffin pulled out their phones to study their copies of the same article.

I perused the article over Tucker's shoulder, but this time, I slowed down to read the prologue.

White Lightning was one sharp dresser. He was always turned out in a soft collar shirt and a suit jacket and no waistcoat. Although some men might look untidy with a soft collar, White Lightning favoured a collar bar to hold the fabric in place without damaging it.

His tie clip was also most unusual to this reporter. He explained that it was solid silver, made in Siam using the Nielloware technique. The figure was created by carving the background out by hand before applying a black chemical mixture that melted during the firing process.

"D'you like Mekkala?" he asked with a big grin, referring to the figure on his tie clip. "She's the goddess of lightning. You won't see her anywhere else. She's one of a kind."

When asked where he might have obtained such a unique piece, he gazed into the distance and said, "From a one of a kind. Are we doing this interview, or what?"

"Check this out." Griffin messaged us a photo. He'd blown up the newspaper picture of White Lightning.

My heart thudded as I recognized White Lightning's tie clip. "Tucker."

"I see it." He could barely get the words out.

Tori turned her dark eyes on us. "What happened?"

"Tucker has that exact tie clip. It was passed down from some sort of uncle."

"A great great uncle Fred," Tucker managed to grind out.

Griffin muttered something that sounded like "Freaky, bro," under his breath. Tori said nothing, her dark eyes on Tucker.

"Tori, do you know if all three brothers served overseas, where they would have gotten that pin?" I asked.

Tori's eyes widened. "No. Only William did. He served as a pilot in Asia."

I nodded. "So William was old enough to have the white hair, he knew how to fly, and he was the only one who would have picked up the pin overseas."

We all sat in silence until I asked Tucker gently, "How did your Great Great Uncle Fred end up with the tie clip?"

I was afraid he might throw up like he had last night. To my surprise, Tucker reached for the leather journal I'd laid on Tori's fake wood tray table. "Let's find out."

63

Tucker read aloud so we could all hear. I read over his shoulder, surveying the author's copperplate, faded ink handwriting for myself.

Sometimes he kisses me and tells me how he can't wait for the baby. I tell him that I can't wait until we are married and legally united under God.

He says that he needs more of a nest egg first. He says that things are different after the Great War and that God will understand. I am not so certain.

Tucker paused after he read that, and he passed it to me. "Maybe you should take over."

I held it up to Tori and Griffin, silently asking if they'd prefer to have the honour. She shook her head and took Griffin's hand. He lifted his chin at me, telling me to go ahead.

For the first 24 hours after a concussion you're supposed to take it easy in a dark room and not read, text or watch movies. I belatedly realized that those rules should apply to Tori too, so I didn't argue with her as I took over the reading.

Sometimes when he talks, he touches his tie clip and smiles. Frances told me that soldiers went to Siam for R&R, and ever since then, the clip has not appeared so innocent. I realize that men have needs. Who knows better than I, after running this inn? Even so, some days, I would like to throw that clip in the Detroit River.

"Gertrud," said Tori softly.

"And White Lightning," said Griffin.

I eyed Tucker silently. He gestured at me to continue.

A big clump of pages seemed to be stuck together. Instead of fighting with them, I flipped to the next page that was easily accessible.

Freddy came to see me today. He said that he and Louis agreed that it wasn't good for me to live alone at the inn.

"I'm hardly alone. I'm constantly surrounded by visitors and waitstaff," I said.

"It's not the same, Trudy. You need someone to look after you."

I knew what he meant. My hand started to drift toward my belly, but I made sure to tighten the apron sash instead of making a protective gesture. Although I've started to wear looser dresses, he has probably suspected for the past month or so. He's a farmer, accustomed to animal husbandry.

"I wonder when Will will come back," I said, as if I were merely making conversation.

He scratched his head. "That's Will for you. You never know."

He smiled at me again. He wanted to tell me that he was reliable, unlike fickle Will. Freddy could take me away from the uncertainties of the Dreamland Inn, to the comfort and security of a farm.

"I have customers to tend to," I said, and hurried away.

How could I explain the satisfaction of my own inn? I know that my debts keep me awake at night, and I hardly have time to sleep even when the little one isn't kicking me, but it means a great deal when every penny that comes in belongs to me, free and clear.

I would die on a farm. The sameness, tied to one square patch of land, one set of demanding animals and crops after another, and frankly, one boring man.

"Fuck," Tucker said out loud. "I wonder if my Great Great Uncle Fred killed my Great Great Uncle Will over 'Trudy.'"

64

I tentatively touched Tucker's rigid neck. He didn't move away. In fact, his muscles relaxed a hair's breadth.

"We don't know for sure," I said, starting to massage him.

He exhaled before he moved away. "I feel like a tool."

I shook my head. Tori did, too, pressing her lips together. Griffin listened in silence as Tucker continued.

"I've been riding you about being a detective doctor, because I need a case of my own. Meanwhile, I missed everything: one ancestor got rich by exploiting other climbing boys. Another one was a bootlegging pilot who might have gotten other pilots killed."

I opened my mouth. They never said what happened to the pilots who crashed. But yes, most likely, they died. I tried to touch his arm.

Tucker evaded me. "And now the crowning achievement. One of my not-so-great uncles might have murdered his brother and stuffed his body up the chimney of the woman he said he loved."

"We all have things we're not proud of in our family history," said Tori.

I turned to her. Her background is Japanese. I don't hold the Rape of Nanking against her, but we'd never talked about what our respective ancestors might have done.

Tori ignored my gaze as she locked eyes with Tucker. "Your history doesn't define you. It's what you do with your life. As long as I've known you, you've tried to help others."

Tucker shook his head. "We're all doctors."

"Not like you," I said. "I don't make friends with residents from Oman and learn how to cook their food. I don't sing with strangers on the street at 2 p.m."

Slowly, his beautiful brown eyes moved to mine. His glistened, choking me up, but I pressed on. "Everyone else I know does what they're supposed to do. Work hard, work out, eat mostly healthy food. They go to bed, they wake up, and it's Groundhog Day. Not you. You're excited if you meet a dog or try skateboarding or read a new paper. You really suck the marrow out of life. You make me appreciate every minute the way I never did before."

"You've also almost died at least nine times," he pointed out.

"Yeah, there's that." We grinned at each other. I blinked ferociously and tried to control my hoarse voice. "But you're so different, so full of life. If you have rotten ancestors, well, okay. I'm not into that. But I love *you*."

He crushed me against his chest, smashing my nose. I twisted my head to the side so I could breathe and snuffle as he whispered, "I love you, Hope."

"I love you, too. And look on the bright side. You're *not* related to Al Capone. I think that was a clue that the brother, not the butler, did it. WL's brother here and the scar for Scarface back then."

Tucker honked out a laugh.

When we finally drew apart, Tori and Griffin were reading the journal, purposely not watching us.

Griffin pointed at something, Tori nodded, and after giving us another minute to make sure we were done, they passed us a letter that had been pressed between the journal's pages.

MY DARLING GIRL,
I've been thinking about what you said the other night.

The great thing about being a pilot is that you never have to worry. If the plane drops, you go unconscious. You never know what happened to you. Doesn't get any better than that, does it? Snuffed out like a candle.

I don't want to be stuck underground like the rest of the corpses. I want to burn up until there's nothing left and fly free forever.

Will you fly with me?

WL

I HELD the letter while emotions warred within me before I turned it over to Tucker. He held the yellowed paper carefully in both hands as he read.

When he was done, I picked up the diary and said, "It's sort of funny that he signed it like that, keeping a fake name even in a love letter. Except I never noticed that the initials for White Lightning was WL. Will, or William. And his real name was John William Tucker. It must have made it easier for him to adopt a pseudonym. Also, he must have loved flying so much."

Tucker touched my hair and gave me a lopsided grin. "I was going to say, he really loved her."

65

We took our time passing the journal so we could each read the final page of writing.

Lord, I know that you want more for me, and I will always serve You. I feel a calling to leave this place. Truth to tell, it has never been right since Will disappeared. Patrons complained of an odour until Freddy completed the renovations.

I gulped and exchanged a look with Tucker, who was reading it in tandem with me. A muscle flexed in his jaw.

Prohibition is over, the kitchen requires still more extensive work, the musicians leave in droves, and most of all, Adelaide.

There was a blotch on the page beside "Adelaide." It might have been a smear of the ink, a tear, or both.

I prayed every night for guidance, and at long last, He has guided me toward a new life in a new city. There are too many memories here of sweet Will and even sweeter Adelaide. I used to sing "Sweet Georgia Brown" to our little girl.

I will leave this book here so that you may find me if you so desire. If I ever had another little girl, I'd call her Marietta. I believe I'm too old for that now, but I remember the story of Isaac and Sarah and I never lose faith.

Lord, we had a good run here. No matter what anyone else says, I believe that You kept me safe from the crooked men who cheated at every turn. You tried to protect me from the worst heartache.

Through Your help and guidance, I will try a new path. I may not be destined for greatness, born too late for Atlantis and too early for justice for poor women like me, but I will try.

MY THROAT TIGHTENED as I passed the book to Griffin, who had lifted his hand to signal that he wanted another look. I said, "She lost baby Adelaide."

Tucker drew me to his side, pressing a kiss on my cheek.

Tori nodded, her eyes wide with sympathy.

"I wonder where Gertrud went," I said, pressing my cheek against Tucker's shoulder. "She made a new life. But what kind of life would she have?"

Griffin reread the pages and lifted the journal's spine toward me. "There's something more to this one."

Tori nodded. "She wrote it in code for Will."

I blinked. "No. What?" I'd skipped past a lot of the religious stuff and might have missed any subtle clues.

Tori touched Griffin's arm affectionately. "I was alerted by the fact that the ink color is darker and her writing is especially neat on this entry. She wanted this one to be read and understood."

Griffin covered her hand with his. "Too bad he wasn't around to get it."

"She probably knew that, but she was covering her bets," Tori told him. "I wouldn't be surprised if she waited here until 1946 because she kept hoping he'd come back, even after Prohibition ended."

Tucker plucked the journal off the bed. "Let me see."

I reread it over his shoulder, but nothing jumped out at me. I gave Tori the side-eye. How could she get electrocuted and go into cardiac arrest, but the next morning, still find more clues than me?

Unless she was more sensitive in general. Like how she'd picked up on Edwin's ghost before she set foot in the door.

As if hearing my thoughts, Tori smiled and hummed a tune that sounded somewhat familiar.

Griffin grinned. Then they both broke into the full-blown version of "Georgia On My Mind," which I recognized because John Legend sang a stirring solo rendition on Twitter after Georgia's votes helped Biden Harris win the 2020 US election.

I applauded, Tucker whistled, and after Tori and Griffin took mini-bows, Tucker said, "You think she went to Georgia because she used to sing 'Sweet Georgia Brown'?"

Tori kissed Griffin's cheek. They were both still beaming from their impromptu singalong. She explained, "That, and then she said Marietta."

Griffin explained, "Marietta, Georgia is a suburb of Atlanta now."

That, I didn't know, but Tori delivered the kicker. "She ended with a side reference: Atlantis is awfully close to Atlanta, don't you think?"

I reread the entry, shaking my head. It seemed packed with clues, now that they'd mentioned it. "I wonder why she went to Marietta. Wasn't she a German immigrant who settled in the Northeastern United States? She could have gone back to Detroit, or New York ... "

"She wanted a new life. I bet she wanted a cheap place to live where she didn't have to stay up all night and deal with drunks," said Tucker. "I don't blame her."

"I get that. I want to get away from people too. Not you," I told Tucker and Tori and Griffin, and I meant it. We'd become a team this weekend.

66

Tucker pressed a kiss on my temple. Griffin gave me a slow nod. And Tori's face lit up with a gentle, forgiving smile that made me love her all over again.

We poked around on our phones for a bit before Griffin said, "I found a Trudy Tucker who worked at a restaurant in Marietta, Georgia in 1949. I wonder."

We all laughed and agreed to look her up.

Tucker cleared his throat. "I still like people. I have to figure out my ancestors, though, and what that means to me. I ordered a genetic testing kit."

We all turned to stare at him.

"Josie and I both agreed to do it," he said. "It'll show if we're relatives. And if my dad and uncles and other relatives do it too ..."

I cautiously reached out to touch his arm. He gave me a half-smile, so I circled his bicep with my fingers. "Is that really what you want?"

He nodded. "I want to know. The only thing worse than being related to reprobates is *not* knowing if you're related for the rest of your life. I want to figure it out and move on."

Tori cleared her throat. "Remember, Josie said her relative was the rich chimney sweep."

"I know." Tucker's brows knitted, and we walked to her bedside, hand in hand.

"If that's true," said Tori, "your common relative was the one who ran out on Edwin Jenkins. Edwin became a climbing boy first, got trapped in a chimney, and died."

"I know." Tucker's hands fisted, squeezing my fingers painfully.

"The other John didn't kill Edwin directly, but he knew exactly what happened to climbing boys. He ran out so that Mr. Bagnell would pick Edwin instead."

"He did," said Tucker. "I'm sorry about that. I mean, it wasn't me, but it might have been my relative. Hell, it might have been me if I'd been born on the other side of the world 200 years ago, poor, and not knowing what to do."

I thought of Cloud. It was so easy to blame others, but who looked after the lost children? The poor ones. The ones with no families. The ones with no school and no second chances.

"If it's any consolation—" Tucker hesitated. "Josie thinks that the reason he took the boat to Canada was that he was haunted."

"By Edwin?" I asked.

Tucker nodded and shrugged at the same time. "I assume so. He heard voices. His wife refused to sleep with him because he'd roll around at night and twitch. Once he punched her in the face and yelled, 'We're dead!'"

Tori gasped. The look in her eyes was so terrible that I turned to Tucker, who seemed stricken as he met her gaze.

Tori's fists clenched. I thought she might levitate out of the bed with frustration. Griffin scrambled to his feet, and after a long moment, she managed to assume her usual reserved mask. Still, the hairs on my arms prickled with unease.

"I'm sorry," said Tucker again, shaking his head. "I know this doesn't help you, or Edwin, but she told me that the other John did kind of lose it. He drank too much, a lot of his investments went sour, and our family's been kind of poor ever since."

The masseter muscles in Tori's jaw relaxed slightly. She sat up in bed and swung her legs over the sides. "I'm not sure why Edwin came to Canada. I think something about WTLNG and the Mackenzie Corporation must have triggered him."

And make him haunt Tori? I didn't pretend to understand this massive puzzle. There are more things in heaven and earth, Horatio.

"Haunts me, too." Tucker rubbed his eyes and left his hands over his face as he said, "I just fuckin' remembered something."

Tucker doesn't swear as much as I do, so we all stared at him.

He whispered into his hands, "Josie was telling me about the rich man on the Grant side of her family."

Josie's health card blazed in my mind: *Josie Sophia Grant Tucker*.

"Fuck!" My hindbrain had tried to remind me last night, before Jennifer interrupted me with this diary. "So you think ... "

"I might *also* be related to the stalker pedophile who tried to throw you off the roof, torture a teenager, electrocute your best friend, and molest your brother."

We all sat in silence. Then I put my arms around Tucker and said, "Then again, you might not."

I felt his body shudder before he looked me dead in the eyes and said, "I probably am. Which made it even more fun for him to set this whole clusterfuck up. Screw you, screw me, screw Ke—"

"Don't go there." I cut him off.

Tori spoke more calmly. "It wasn't you."

"I don't know how closely related—"

"No!" Tori's shout filled the room. She started to cough, and Griffin quickly poured her a glass of water from the sink.

She took the plastic cup and sipped it slowly. Tucker moved toward the bed, and I followed him, taking his hand.

We clustered around her until she handed Griffin back the cup, mouthed her thanks, and told Tucker, "I don't care who you're related to. You're not your great great uncle's keeper. You probably never met Frederick Grant before today, or if you did, it was only because he was stalking you and Hope. That's on him. What matters is your actions, not your blood."

Tucker shook his head and opened his mouth.

She held up her hand to silence him. "I know you have to work through this on your own. It may take a long time, even a lifetime."

I hugged Tucker one-armed. I'd be here for him. He leaned into me, only a touch, but enough to lift my heart.

Tori nodded slightly. "I want you to know this. Whether or not you believe in ghosts, Edwin's gone now. As far as I can tell, he disappeared after he helped bring lightning down on Frederick Grant."

"But—"

Tori shut Tucker down. "He struck *Frederick Grant* with a bolt of lightning. Not you. It had nothing to do with you. And then Edwin left."

We all mulled that over. If you believed Tori—and there was something quietly compelling about her, even though I couldn't sense ghosts—then Edwin had passed judgement on the perpetrator. Who wasn't Tucker.

In fact, maybe Edwin helped electrocute Combover Guy while he was at it.

Zap zap! I almost smiled, except *jamais deux sans trois*. Tori had almost died too. She was innocent. And she was helping Edwin. He should have protected Tori if he'd been able.

No, I couldn't make any supernatural sense out of this one. Maybe ghosts can wreak justice and bring the heavens down on someone, or maybe electric current had flowed according to the laws of physics and no more.

I pushed everything out of my head except the fact that two horrid human beings had been taken down last night, and we'd saved the life of one of the best people in the world, now lying in front of me.

And another of the best people standing beside me. I kissed Tucker's cheek. He leaned into it more obviously this time, reminding me of Ryan's dog, Roxy the Rottweiler. I smiled and blinked back tears of my own.

Griffin rubbed Tori's back. "Maybe Edwin's at peace now, babe."

She leaned against him and closed her eyes. "I think so. I pray for that."

We all sat in a spontaneous moment of silence for Edwin until a bird called outside the hospital, a series of quick peeps that made us all smile.

"I love you," I told Tori. "I never told you, but you're one of my best friends."

She smiled at me from Griffin's arms. "Even though I'm stupid enough to get electrocuted?"

I didn't know whether to laugh or cry. "You couldn't help the fact that the waterbed leaked. The police said that his electric blanket and phone charger were both frayed. I guess he was putting too much coin into his *picana* and not enough into maintaining the rest of his equipment."

Tucker barked out a laugh that made me grin, too, although I said, "Not his sexual equipment. His blanket. Oh, you know what I mean."

Tucker squeezed my hand. I knew he hadn't forgiven me for how I felt about Ryan, but he still loved me, and I loved him. That was something.

Maybe it was even enough.

Tori's closed her eyes. Griffin guided her back into bed, tucking the sheets around her, and she didn't stop him. She murmured, "I was trying to be like you."

"What?"

"You know. Brave. To boldly go."

"What?" My stomach clenched with guilt. Tori almost died because she was imitating *me?*

"I'll never do it again." She closed her eyes, her lovely eyelashes casting a shadow on her cheeks.

"Promise," Griffin whispered, although she already seemed to have slipped into sleep.

I swore to myself, under my breath. "Don't be like me, Tori. Be yourself."

She might have smiled. The curve of her lips reminded me of

Frederick Grant's face mask, and I stilled, willing that mask out of my mind.

I concentrated on Tori's lovely face, and eventually the white mask faded from my consciousness. Tori's chest rose and fell evenly. Edwin's ghost might finally have gone in peace, and she could rest.

Griffin stroked her hair. "She told me you all were crazy. I said I could handle it."

I gulped.

His eyes narrowed. "I don't want to handle any more."

"No. Me neither," I assured him.

Griffin's nostrils flared. He didn't look convinced.

"I'm going to live a quiet life," said Tucker. "My biggest excitement will be the genetic testing." His eyes moved between me, Tori, and Griffin, his expression set. "I wanted adventure, but maybe I need to go back to my roots. That's good enough for now."

Tucker? Swearing off of mysteries? I'd believe it when I saw it. But I was familiar with wanting calm and contentment instead of wild adventures. I squeezed his hand and tucked my nose into his shoulder, breathing his sweat and cologne.

Maybe, like Gertrud, we could build a new and better life for ourselves. Maybe we could still love and forgive each other.

At least it was enough for us to go forth for another day.

We sat in Tori's room, watching her breathe, with the steady display of her cardiac monitor tracing lighting up the room. Normal sinus rhythm, 78 beats per minute.

It was one of the most beautiful things I'd ever seen in my entire life.

ACKNOWLEDGMENTS

It all started with the woman who offered to make Hope her own gin. That made me research alcohol and crime. Did you know that in 1734, a woman called Judith Dufour killed her toddler so that she could sell his clothes for gin?

I didn't get that dark. However, Edwin's story does come close, thanks to Niels van Manen's excellent Ph.D. thesis, *The Climbing Boy Campaigns in Britain, c. 1770-1840: Cultures of Reform, Languages of Health and Experiences of Childhood*.

I began with a kernel in George Brown College's playwriting class, taught by Rosamund Small. My classmates were invaluable, particularly Rashmi Biswas.

Rashmi portrayed Edwin in the Winnipeg Fringe version of Edwin's tale. It's a Lego stop action piece at https://www.youtube.com/watch?v=uHFk9FSUKYk at 1:17:37, where you can also admire voice acting by Andy Phypers and Sally Phypers, and some stop action by Anastasia Innes.

I'm indebted to Charles Henry "Mary" Gervais's *The Rumrunners: A Prohibition Scrapbook*. The White Lightning character was inspired by King Canada (Blaise Diesbourg), and Gertrud Adams was influenced by Bertha Thomas, who owned the Edgewater Thomas Inn.

Mark Leslie told me about ghosts. r/AskReddit gave me Cloud's costume, Blue Guy, and the fire at https://bit.ly/3zycp37. Sean Young helped me hammer out the plot. BAFERD Canadian and U.S. emergency doctors made some electric suggestions.

I considered Montreal for its history of both bootlegging and jazz, Chicago for the Capone connection, Detroit, and Cincinnati, but in the end, it had to be Windsor.

Un gros merci à Johanne Brassard et la Maison du Bootlegger in Charlevoix. Visiting one of Quebec's last remaining Prohibition buildings gave me some critical details for the setting of the Rumrunner's Rest. La Maison's table d'hôte is exquisite, the staff kind, the tour important, and you can rock out at 9:30 pm. Make sure you have a formal reservation for dinner to get a tour.

Alessandro Baricco wrote in *An Iliad*, "*...porque no hay nada en la faz de la tierra, nada que respire o camine, nada tan infeliz como lo es el hombre.*" "He fell to the ground like an olive tree ... " sounds elegant in Italian.

Sarah Hosking, Lexie Conyngham, and Kathleen Costa helped me with historical and writing details. Emergency physicians in Canada and the US advised me on electrocution. All errors are my own.

Grateful to S, B, N, and M for your feedback, Margaret for editing, Maggie for her support at Windtree, Pierre L'Allier for communication, and Mickey Mikkelson and Beverly Bambury for publicity.

Thanks to my long-suffering husband for his insight, and my children for their patience. I didn't realize I had to reserve lodging and meals separately at la Maison du Bootlegger, so they ended up eating pizza instead of steak. But they still love me.

If you enjoyed this book, please let a friend know. Massive thanks for posting an online review, because it's so hard to reach new readers. I also super appreciate if you sign up for my KamikaSze mailing list in exchange for a free gift. And with any luck, you'll be able to purchase White Lightning from Gin*Eco*Logic starting in the next year or two.

This is a trying time for all compassionate people. I'll end with a quote from Dolly Parton: "I make a point to appreciate all the little things in my life. I go out and smell the air after a good, hard rain."

Wishing all of you fresh air and clean water and challenging yet refreshing books as we move into the future.

ABOUT THE AUTHOR

Melissa Yi is an emergency doctor with an award-winning writing career.

She believes in science, kindness, and friendship.

Get the rumble by joining the KamikaSze newsletter on Melissa's website, www.myi.ninja. You'll earn a free Hope novella

If you think White Lightning's the bee's knees, post a review for the other cats before you dust out.

- amazon.com/author/myi
- facebook.com/MelissaYiYuanInnes
- twitter.com/dr_sassy
- bookbub.com/authors/melissa-yi
- instagram.com/melissa.yuaninnes
- pinterest.com/melissayi_

ALSO BY MELISSA YI

Flamingo Flamenco (Hope Sze short story)

Code Blues (Hope Sze 1)

Notorious D.O.C. (Hope Sze 2)

Family Medicine (essay & Hope Sze novella combining the short stories *Cain and Abel, Trouble and Strife, and Butcher's Hook*, which are also available separately or as a newsletter subscription gift)

Terminally Ill (Hope Sze 3)

Student Body (Hope Sze novella post-Terminally Ill; includes radio drama *No Air*)

Blood Diamonds (Hope Sze short story)

The Sin Eaters (Hope Sze short story)

Stockholm Syndrome (Hope Sze 4)

Human Remains (Hope Sze 5) (Hope Sze 5)

Blue Christmas (Hope Sze short story)

Death Flight (Hope Sze 6)

Graveyard Shift (Hope Sze 7)

Scorpion Scheme (Hope Sze 8)

White Lightning (Hope Sze 9)

More mystery & romance novels by Melissa Yi

The Italian School for Assassins *(Octavia & Dario Killer School Mystery 1)*

The Goa Yoga School of Slayers *(Octavia & Dario Killer School Mystery 2)*

Wolf Ice

High School Hit List

The List

Dancing Through the Chaos

Unfeeling Doctor Series (Melissa Yuan-Innes)

The Most Unfeeling Doctor in the World and Other True Tales From the Emergency Room (Unfeeling Doctor #1)

The Unfeeling Doctor, Unplugged: More True Tales From Med School and Beyond (Unfeeling Doctor #2)

The Unfeeling Wannabe Surgeon: A Doctor's Medical School Memoir (Unfeeling Doctor #3)

The Unfeeling Thousandaire: How I Made $10,000 Indie Publishing and You Can, Too! (Unfeeling Doctor #4)

Buddhish: Exploring Buddhism in a Time of Grief: One Doctor's Story (Unfeeling Doctor #5)

The Unfeeling Doctor Betwixt Birthing Babies: Poems About Love, Loss, and More Love (Unfeeling Doctor #6)

The Knowledgeable Lion: Poems and Prose by the Unfeeling Doctor in Africa (Unfeeling Doctor #7)

Fifty Shades of Grey's Anatomy: The Unfeeling Doctor's Fresh Confessions from the Emergency Room (Unfeeling Doctor #8)

Broken Bones: New True Noir Essays From the Emergency Room by the Most Unfeeling Doctor in the World (Unfeeling Doctor #9)

The Emergency Doctor's Guide Series (Melissa Yuan-Innes)

The Emergency Doctor's Guide to a Pain-Free Back: Fast Tips and Exercises for Healing and Relief

The Emergency Doctor's Guide to Healing Dry Eyes